THE OTHERSIDE OF ATLAS

Devon
Scott
Fagan

The Otherside of Atlas Copyright © 2019 by Devon Scott Fagan. All Rights Reserved.

All rights reserved. No part of this book may be reproduced in any form or by any electronic or mechanical means including information storage and retrieval systems, without permission in writing from the author. The only exception is by a reviewer, who may quote short excerpts in a review.

Cover designed by Adubiaro Opeyemi Samuel

Edited by Heather Tippett-Wertz, Megan Lamb, Carly Schankowitz, and Devon Scott Fagan

This book is a work of fiction. Names, characters, places, and incidents either are products of the author's imagination or are used fictitiously. Any resemblance to actual persons, living or dead, events, or locales is entirely coincidental.

Devon Scott Fagan
Visit my website at www.devonfagan.weebly.com

Printed in the United States of America

First Printing: Feb 2019
Amazon KDP

ISBN 9781796388855

TO MOA,

And everyone else who helped to make my dreams a reality.

And Julia.

Thank you for getting me through this year! I hope you enjoy, Love. Tell me what you think!

Hit me up for tattics.

♥

Place your hand over your heart. Feel that? It's called purpose. You're alive for a reason. Don't give up.
—JOYCE MEYER

THE CYCLOPS

His sole menacing eye stares back at me, darkened, black like the death he brings. A Cyclops. A tear runs down my face, followed by another. This cyclops has lived under my bed for some time now, waiting to make his grand appearance. I could only look into his eye for a split second at a time before pulling away. Even after thinking about him for so long, his mystery and the unknown he brings scares me. He's misunderstood though. He could take the pain away. All I had to do was say yes. I set him down in the corner for now. Away from *our* box of memories.

I can't focus. Why can't I focus? All I can think about is *him*. I'm not behind the controls anymore. I am a spectator. I can't stop thinking about *him*. How it felt to look into that eye. The knot in my stomach grows tighter, and I'm becoming antsier. I know what is going to happen, but I ignore it, staring too long into the eye of my inevitable fate. Nobody wants me, or at least that's what I keep telling myself. Yes, my family wants me of course, at least I hope, but isn't that such a cliche? However, the thought of nobody wanting me might be an even bigger cliché.

Everybody has somebody. My parents love me, it may be rocky, but this is undeniable. I have camera rolls of memories, scrapbooks ready to be filled, and a contact list, arguably as diverse as a phone book. However, at this point, 1:39 A.M., I am painfully alone. The lump in my throat has become concrete. I just want to run away, but each tear that falls tightens my chain. My slack is disappearing. I just want freedom and peace inside of my own head.

With each minute that passes, more intense heat rolls over my body. I'm now in a full-on sweat. My body enters fight or flight mode, except I am the only danger in the room.

God, if you are here, I don't beg for your forgiveness because I know my pain is the product of my destructive lifestyle, all my own doing. I plead you show mercy to the mind of anybody else anchored to this kind of pain.

My nose is raw, and my left sleeve soaked with snot. My mind is running left, and then right, doing 360s, the patterns are unpredictable. I give

myself a stern slap, like something out of a
movie. This does little to slow down my thoughts.
I get up from my cocoon of blankets and roll off
of my bed. Convincing myself to move, left foot
in front of the right, I walk to the bathroom door
connected to my room. With every step I can feel
my heart pulsing throughout my body, A strange
static-like tingling is sent into each of my limbs. I
rest my head against the door. I can feel its
wooden grooves imprinting on my face. It's good
to know I'm still human and capable of feeling.
I force a promise to myself that I'll calm down
when I walk through this door, even if I know it's
the whitest of lies. I step through the doorway
expecting to be blindly hit with a sense of relief.
Instead, I sob more at the disappointment. I'm
crying so hard, that it's become hard to fit
breathes in between the wails.
I flip the light switch.
What stands in front of me can only be described
as foreign.
I grab the towel rack to my left and hang on,
afraid I'll faint out of fear that the woman, or I
should say child, I'm looking at is me.
Another hard wave crashes into me.
You'd think my constant flow of tears would be
enough to combat the choking heat filling my
chest. I am now begging for mercy. Trying to find
humor in my situation, I boot out a fake giggle,
thankful that I didn't bother putting on any

makeup yesterday. *He* would've laughed at this too.

I look at the clock again. 1:43 A.M.

The amount of emotions I've fit into the last 4 minutes is somewhat amazing. The sole neon picture frame sitting on my sink grabs my eye and won't free it. I dare not look at the photograph. That would just be asking for more of this. At the bottom written in glitter and sequences is "Blake +" but my eyes refuse to register the name after that. I am thankful. I clamber out of the bathroom, smacking my toe off of the door, paying it no mind.

Lying dead center in the middle of my shag carpet, staring up into the light above me, I tell myself that I'm going to try to sleep. But deep down I know I'm not safe there. *He* would be there. Smiling. Making me laugh. Apologizing. That would be too much for me right now.

I remember reading somewhere that if you stay perfectly still for ten minutes you'll fall asleep. For me, the girl who got up in five or ten-minute intervals to fakely blow my nose or get hand sanitizer in class, to sit perfectly still for that long is nothing short of impossible. I took a deep breath. The war was still waging on upstairs.

I made one of those dumb promises to God. You know, the ones you make when you're about to get arrested or in a life or death situation. It goes like "*God, I promise on everything I love that if you get me out of this, I will start reading the bible more, and I'll donate money to charity and do something nice for my parents, and..."* so on and so on.

If it comes through usually you make good on your end of the deal for a week or so until you forget or until the next time you have to cut a deal with the man upstairs. This one used the same standard format but was tweaked with the wish of just blessing me with unconsciousness.

All I want is to just not have to think; I don't care how long it's for. I would be grateful for even a half hour. I would be grateful for five minutes. Just shut me off. No more thoughts about *him*, no thoughts about tomorrow or the day after that. I'm vulnerable and if God wanted, he could really take advantage of me. I snap my head to the giant plastic bin covered with John Mayer and Star Wars stickers sitting on my nightstand.

That's right, Jesus.

The whole piggy bank to the next homeless man under the bridge. You have my word. Thirty minutes. Just shut off my thoughts. Please. I start weeping. It's no use, you can't fake cry in front of God.

My phone reads 1:47. Time is passing painfully slow. I wasted four more minutes pleading to a ghosty man high in the sky, at this point I was realizing my prayer was not coming true. I instantly thought of what I'd done wrong in the last couple days that angered him enough to not help me at a time like this. Fully soaked with sweat, I took my shirt off and sling shot it across the room, just missing the overflowing hamper full of laundry I was supposed to tackle days ago. I wasn't hot anymore; I was just basking in the aftermath of it. I ran my hands up and down my arms trying to squeegee the sweat off of me. After this, I rolled around on my carpet to get it off my back. It struck me that for the last couple minutes my mind had cooled off. The armies of each half of my brain must have called a cease-fire to see who would make the next move.

Jesus, what am I doing? Maybe he was up there watching over me. God, I mean. I was cooling off and calming down again. I got up off of the floor. So much for sitting still for ten minutes, but it was okay. Knowing I might start feeling a little better was giving me a boost. I didn't feel like absolutely nothing anymore. I didn't exactly feel like anything special, but I did feel like something. Which, respectively, is much better than the nothingness I was just feeling. My thoughts were hard to navigate, almost like smoke was just being pumped into my head. It was hard to control what I was thinking or get away from them. It was hard to get away because I was begging to feel anything at all. I wanted to know I was still alive and human. I'm going to stop myself right here, I feel like trying to think anything at all would pretty much be like skipping through a minefield. One wrong move and boom, I would be overtaken, reduce to a vegetable rolling around on the floor, tears and drool mixed together covering my vegetable face. My best bet is surviving until morning. I settled down and took a quick glance around my room, ranking the possibilities in the order that I'll pursue them. None, however, took the starting spot. I could do all that laundry. Actually no, not a chance. Miss Josefina, the maid, comes tomorrow and she'll do it for me.

Tommy Lee, my teddy bear of a father, always gets mad when I call her a maid. She's here so often that he's always pushing me to call her something like "Aunt J" to make her feel at home. I think that's a little too corny though.

I could always read. I wouldn't mind volunteering to be whisked away into a universe of ink and printed paper. Anywhere that my problems aren't center of attention will do. Currently, *The Beautiful and Damned* is sitting untouched on my nightstand, making a nice coaster for my jar of funds. I'd call myself a Fitzgerald fan, but starting a new journey and trying to attach myself to strange uncharted territories and stories doesn't sound appealing right now. I want to just hop back into one of my hundred pre-existing lives on my bookshelf.

I don't dare touch *Gatsby*.

My green light was already burning through its last bit of fuel at an alarming rate. While I stood by, questioning if it was worth it to fill back up. I don't know if it was mentally possible to refuel. Nonetheless, my light was taking its final buoyant breaths.

Collecting a stockpile of dust next to *The Great Gatsby* was a copy of *For Whom the Bell Tolls* by Ernest Hemingway. It kills me to say but I haven't read much of his work. A flash of my English teachers room dropped into my head. There it was. The sign hanging on his wall, encasing an ever so brilliant idea. "Write hard and clear about what hurts." How has the idea eluded me for this long?

Usually writing stupid scrappy poems is how I deal with my anxiety attacks. I wrote a little bit earlier, but I can't call the writing I had done earlier a piece of my own work, because the real author behind my controls was unknown. A different person wrote those poems. A broken woman full of broken thoughts. We essentially are the same except, now, I am in control. At this very moment, I am free; I'm taking back the controls. I'm making the choice. That is, until my ruthless captors choose to yank back my chain, exposing my lack of power for the facade that it is.

Why didn't I think about this earlier? Considering I know just as much as anyone else about where

my life has gone in the last year, this could be a
chance to see from an outside perspective. I
started sweating lightly. I wasn't overheating, I
was just nervous. It was such a great idea. I'll tell
it all. The entire thing. Nobody needs to ever read
it except for me. I never thought I'd be writing my
own Playboy tell-all interview. This is what I
need though, to skim over my life with a fresh set
of eyes and some new soles on my feet.

I don't call it a journal or a diary. That just leaves
an embarrassing taste in my mouth. More like a
ballad, a true and ingenious testimony of what
drove me into this scorched place. I wanted to do
this.

After clearing all of the dark poems and random
jot downs of littered feelings from earlier, I had
before me an empty canvas. I hunkered down on
my bed, preparing myself for what was about to
follow. I grabbed my trusty dark blue pen, my go-
to writing utensil for any late night study or
homework sessions, it's the one *he* left at my
house the first time he came over to do
homework.

It was a strange thing knowing minutes ago I was
struggling to purge these painfully penetrating
thoughts from my head, and now I'm seconds
away from making note of every individual one
of them. A heavy weight washed over me, and a
brisk sweat brewed from my arms. I didn't even

bother to put any clothes on, an acknowledgment I was only going to get worse.

I took the deepest of breaths, filling every corner of my lungs with air. Out it went. Along with it went the dark acknowledgement that when I looked in the mirror earlier, I really didn't know who I was. Surely I looked the same. The eyes weren't mine, however. The body matched up, but the eyes, previously filled with awe and love, were completely drained. Being sucked dry, day by day, until they had nothing left and withered away into the dust. I don't deserve to be here. I looked around my room. Fit for a queen. I didn't deserve any of it.

I grabbed my phone and clicked on the lock screen on. 1:59.

I shut off my phone along with the hatred for myself which I had stockpiled in every nook, cranny, and cavern of my body I could store it in and grabbed my freshly purged notebook. When I write, it gives me an escape. It was like literary paradise for my choking conscious. Except this wasn't going to be me basking in acceptance that I was a shitty person, no no no, I wouldn't let it be that. Everybody deserves a second chance. I remember reading about a man named Frank Abagnale, who had served five years in prison for writing false checks. He cut a deal with the government to help them sniff out other crooks and now he runs a fraud consulting company.

After doing so much wrong in the world, people still saw the good in him as a person. They let him escape his demons. Now, obviously I didn't write 2.5 million dollars' worth of false checks and pretend to be a lawyer, doctor, and an airplane pilot, but in my heart, it is like I had committed crimes much worse. I don't deserve a clean slate, but at the same time, nobody should have to live with this thick fog in your head, slowing down any means of navigating through your thoughts and emotions. My control station had been hijacked by agony and this notebook was my militia of freedom fighters. I clicked my blue, probably purple, pen and touched it to the paper, ready to write *my* side to the story. Pure and unedited, no guilt to interfere.

CHAPTER ONE

Stains congregated around the thighs on my jeans. I kept wiping my hands on them but they wouldn't stop sweating and sweating and sweating. I kept telling myself to take deep breaths, but even my breathing was beyond my control now. Tommy Lee pulled up to the curb. "Alright we're here," he said. He looked at me for some kind of response. I gave him nothing. Not that I was trying to be disrespectful, but because I was just lost in my own head. His words went right through me with almost no acknowledgment.

"You'll be fine", he assured me. "Just go to the office, and they'll help you find your new classes. You're likable; just smile and make friends."

Still, he got nothing from me. My head felt heavy, my vision seemed to be closing in on itself. I retreated into an infant state; I just wanted to curl up in a ball and cease to exist.

"Hey!" he snapped at me to get my attention. I'm now listening but I refused to look up at him, the tears were a moment from bursting through.

"I grew up here, it's a great school and a great city. I had a lot of fun and met some great people too, people like Kenny. How 'bout you look at this like a blessing? You get to start over, to reinvent yourself."

This may have been true, but I wanted nothing to do with the truth. I wanted home. This was not it.

Finally, he kicked me out of the car; he knew I would've pouted there until the dismissal bell if he hadn't. I watched the Lincoln pull away, taking with it my breath. I felt myself gasping. Was I being a baby? Yes. Did I care? Not at all. I mustered up the courage to turn away from the curb, and there it sat, the entrance to Park Pendleton High School. My eyes rolled over the letters sitting on top of the doors, and I gagged.

Kids rolled in waves past me and up the grand set of steps towards the front doors. Strangely, it was nothing like my old high school, but it was everything a high school should be. The group of preps with colorful shorts and polos has already passed me up, now walking through the large set of six glass doors. To the right of the doors sitting on the edge of the planters, looks to me as what could only be described as emo kids, rare and mythical creatures I'd only ever heard of up to that point. My school didn't really have many kids to fall into this category or any categories at all, but from the abundance of high school dramas I'd seen, they fit the cliché. Headphones hanging around the neck, a cloud of cancerous smoke being blown from the mouths of four out of the six kids. Disgusting. They looked like people whose breath, along with their black hoodies and skinny jeans, undoubtably reeked of nicotine.

"Move your ass," was mumbled aggressively into my ear as I was slightly redirected out from in front of a group of tall boys who were dressed head to toe in athletic gear. I spotted a few letterman jackets in the group of boys. I could tell the boy wasn't trying to push me hard, but he wanted me out of the way. To his defense, I was standing there for a good minute looking lost as could be.

"She's not bad though," muttered one of the boys from the inner cluster. To be quite honest, I blushed. In my mind, there's no such thing as bad attention, especially on my first day.
A stick in the mud no more, against my will, I forced my left foot in front of my right, all the way up to the front doors. I could feel every head turn, their eyes fixed on the outsider who didn't belong. When I picked up my head to look around, however, nobody was staring at me, not a

single glare in my direction. I wiped my hands for what I told myself would be the last time and walked through the great glass doors, telling myself as I passed through those doors, a different me would sprout. Whether I wanted to accept it, my father was right. This was a fresh start, a chance for me to keep my head down and finish senior year without drama and distractions. A hundred and some days and the chains would be off.

The great glass doors led directly into another set of six, much less grand, glass doors with metal detectors and tables set alongside them to slide your book bags and belongings across. This was the first metal detector I had ever walked through, and I was excited to walk through it in a weird way. My former school had no such things. In fact, had I stayed at Richmont Carmel High, I would have graduated in a class of only one hundred and twenty five kids.

Next was locating the office, which was going to be next to impossible without asking for help. I had seen a few approachable girls in the main lobby that the metal detector doors dumped me into. The lobby was a large room lined with trophy displays and anti-drug posters, everything one would expect from a high school. There were two staircases on opposite sides of the room leading up to an overlooking terrace. The students were all filling up the steps so I did the same. One thing I learned quickly was when in Rome, do not step on the heels of somebody's shoes.

"What the hell?" a boy no bigger than me and much, much scrawnier snapped around quickly.

"I'm so sorry," I let out, hoping not to start trouble before the bell rang on my first day of school. He neither accepted nor declined my apology, instead falling out of line to put his foot back in his shoe. I was a nervous wreck. Realizing this only brought on a wave of heat, pouring over my body, making me sweat worse.

I got up to the top of the stairs and was greeted by a mob of different groups of people all standing around talking. Kids talking loud, followed by kids talking louder to drown out the others made it very disorientating. This was most likely where everyone had come to hang out and meet with friends before class. There were a few vending machines in the corner with what looked more like a pile than a line of people in front of it, fighting to get up to the machines. Half of the line I followed was dispersing into their smaller friend groups, while the other half mobbed down the corridor where lockers and classroom doors lined the walls as far as the eye could see.

I could feel the sweat creeping down my sides and lower back. Thinking about how badly I was sweating just amplified it. This added another worry to my list. Right underneath *finding the office while minimizing how stupid I looked* sat *don't stink*. I trotted down the hall behind the pack with my arms slightly out to my sides trying to air out my pits, no doubt leaving a slug-like trail of perspiration on the ground behind me. I forced down another deep breath and started looking around to find the most approachable girl I could find. I sized up a slightly larger girl standing at her locker with a polka dotted sweater that was probably bought by her mother's influence. As I went to make my move, I felt a firm hand on my shoulder, followed by an "Excuse me, miss." I turned around to see an outstretched arm attached to a tall man.

"And you, I assume are our newest student, am I wrong?"

I answered with an anxious "yes."

"Ah, Miss Huston, we're very excited to welcome you to our school!"

My nerves fought back the urge to correct him. Not Huston. It was Hutton, Blake Hutton.

"Have you found the office, or are you still looking for it? Or are you just getting a quick look at our school?"

His teeth were something out of a movie. I'm confident I could have seen my reflection in his pristine top row if I'd looked hard enough.

"Yes..," I said again.

"Yes? Yes, you found the office?"

"No, I'm sorry, I need to find the office."

He let out a small, low laugh, "Not a problem dear, just follow me."

He seemed very genuine. I could tell he was not faking his kindness towards me. I followed his pinstriped suit back to the large room with the vending machines, it had mostly cleared out. We went down one of the sets of stairs. He greeted one of the school police officers in the lobby with a warm "good morning" before turning left into the main hallway that split the two stair sets and ran underneath the terrace from which we came down. I hadn't even noticed the hallway earlier when I came in. We continued on while he asked me vague questions about myself, what I liked to do, what my favorite subject was, and if I would be joining any clubs or sports. I was loosening up slowly, and I didn't feel as anxious anymore. He turned to me quickly.

"Where are my manners? I never introduced myself. Here you are walking with what seems to be a strange, strange man asking you questions, following him without voicing a single suspicion! Well, what does that say about you?"

I knew he was joking, so I let out a small laugh.

"I," he started, "am Dr. Dawson, your principal, as you might have guessed from the suit. Not many other people here will be this dressed up. We allow a very relaxed dress code for our teachers here, I promise."

He spoke in such a crisp and confident manner that I had no trouble believing he had narrated dramatic movie trailers in a past life. I do remember my dad mentioning his name this morning. I told him that, and he looked at me and let out an "mhmm".

"If you don't mind me prodding some more, where was it again your family moved from?"

This was prodding though and struck a nerve with me. I reminded myself that he was just making small talk.

"Well, it's just me and my father… and our cleaning lady if you count her as family." Which honestly I had, I'd known Miss Josefina for about four years now. She had done her best to fill in places where my mother should but was lacking.

"But I used to go to Richmont Carmel."

"Really? Interesting. That's a rather small town over there, isn't it? I bet you knew every bit about every other kid there," he said with his words breaking off into a chuckle at the end.

Except he was right. It was nice to know about everyone else and keep up on the gossip. It wasn't so nice, however, when the tables were turned on you. Word spreads fast in small towns.

We had reached the office at the far end of the corridor. Right before we walked in, his cell phone began to ring. He checked and instantly a look of disappointment dominated his face.

"I have to take this, dear, although I really wish I didn't. In the office, one of our student ambassadors is waiting for you. She has your schedule and your locker combination, everything you'll need to get on your feet, and she'll get you to your first class today. I'm sure you'll fit right in."

I didn't know what to say besides, "Thanks."

"It was a pleasure meeting you, Miss Huston. If you need anything, anything at all just, drop by my office right across the hall," he said with his hand pointing over his shoulder.

He moved swiftly down the hallway, a man with a place to be. As his impeccable style, tortoiseshell glasses, and smell of aftershave left the hallway, I felt somewhat disappointed. I would've liked for him to have given me a tour of the school or shown me to my class. He seemed all too nice for no reason, and I began to wonder how he did it. Walking into the office, I was greeted by a girl holding a folder with my name on it. It had clearly read "Blake Hutton," so I questioned if Dr. Dawson had even bothered to look at it. Her hair was braided back her head, a jean skirt graced her legs, and she had on a checkered Vans shirt. She seemed like a classic soul captured and reincarnated into the wrong time period.

"Hey!" She said introducing herself. "My name is Liv. Well, it's Olivia Books. I'm with you in first period."

I asked her if she would be with me all day, and she told me that she'd walk with me up until fourth period. After that, I would go to lunch and then be on my own for the last three periods of the day. Next, we were on our way to first period, Chemistry.

I noticed I had calmed down and wasn't sweating as much, if at all. As we walked to first period, I figured out more and more of her from each thing she said. We pretty much had cut and pasted my earlier conversation with Dr. Dawson, except she shared parts of herself too, and it was much more informal.

By the time we had reached class, I was sure I had her figured out. I had embarrassingly forgotten her name and asked one more time before we entered the room. She was Olivia Books. She was the kind of girl who stayed up late scrolling through Tumblr and Pinterest. She was definitely a feminist and a strong one at that. She woke up early to get ready, and her daily struggles consisted of choosing which band t-shirt she would wear. She seemed like the kind of girl I could get along with though, so I did my best to befriend her.

My first period was a Chemistry class with Mr. Ravensworth. As Olivia and I walked into the class, the resemblance was all too clear. Mr. Ravensworth was a tall man, well over 6'3," with caramel colored skin and a nose that resembled a beak. He bolted across the room to shake my hand and introduce me to the class.

"What a pleasure to meet you, Miss Huston!" extending his arm towards me. I shook his hand. He asked me if there was anything I would like to share with the class about myself. Although I did want to share the correct pronunciation of my name, I reluctantly said no and then took my seat at the back of the class. By the grace of God, I was given the best seat in the house. I was sitting behind a boy in a letterman jacket who looked way too old for high school. The kind of guys you see in the movies about high school where all of the kids are played by actors at least twenty-three and are way more attractive than physically possible at this age. To my right was my new guardian angel, Olivia. I thanked her for walking me to class.

The Raven then proceeded to ask me a couple of questions about my interests in the field of science. My answer to all of which was a half-assed smile and me rephrasing "not really" or "no" in as many ways as I had to. I didn't enjoy everyone turned around in their seats watching me answer and listening to me while he asked. My goal of the day was just to make it to 2:50 while minimizing the nervously generated sweat stains under my armpits. I was not here to fill out vocal surveys while everyone watched. Next question was my favorite subject since I "majorly lacked any interests in the sciences," I answered "English." The raven rolled his eyes and proceeded to the next scheduled question.

He asked what my plans were after senior year. Raven was not pleased by my simple but honest answer of "I don't know" suggesting that maybe by the end of the year his class would rub off on me and give me an idea for future schooling endeavors.

The rest of class sailed by smoothly. We had taken notes and then Mr. Ravensworth gave us a few minutes before the end of class to socialize. "Please, everyone, find a minute to introduce yourself to Miss Blake Huston, and make her feel welcome," he encouraged. The roguishly handsome letterman turned around to talk to Olivia before he turned to me and introduced himself as Mikey Pierropollesko. "Everyone just calls me Mikey P though." Every douchebag alarm and warning rang out through my head, but his illuminating white teeth shushed them. He was cute. Very cute.

I was, for the most part, calmed down from the waves of anxiety I had that morning, but as the bell rang and Olivia told me that Mikey P was going to walk me to second period, the anxiety had come full circle. Here we go again.

CHAPTER TWO

Mikey and I set off into the wild and lawless wasteland of Park Pendleton High's hallways. It was everything you've seen in the movies: mobs of girls walking down the halls, no doubt shit talking every person they laid their snobby eyes on, and the always awkward PDA couples who lock tongues with each other before each class like the boy is getting shipped off to fight against the Axis powers.

It was actually quite great, and I was beginning to settle in. It was my first day, but I didn't see any major red flags.

Mikey was very nice, despite the ungodly douchey persona given off just by his overwhelmingly sharp jawline and letterman jacket. He gave me the crash course on all the ins and outs and losers and popular kids and party spots and avoid at all cost hoodrat zones.

After walking for what seemed like an eternity—due to the mile-long hallways and four levels to the school, we reached my second period class. Calculus. Shit.

In fact, I had looked over my schedule earlier in first period and nothing alarmed me about calculus until I met my teacher. About the exact opposite of Mr. Ravensworth, Dr. Leeland was nothing less than a garden gnome of a woman with wide open eyes that were only magnified by the 1950's wire-framed spectacles from which her piercing eyes looked through.

"And what is your name?" she asked. Mikey giggled and gave me a "Good luck," that made Dr. Leeland's gaze snap to him.

"Excuse me, Mr. Pierropollesko?"

"I'm gonna take my seat now," he said as the few other kids who got here before us laughed. I joined in, pissing her off even more.

"Since you're joining us so late in the year, I'll make sure to put you right up front to help catch you up, wouldn't want to be behind now would we?" Pausing to see if I would argue and dig my already dug hole much deeper. "And what did you say your name was?"

"Blake Hutton."

"Well then Miss Huston, take your seat. My name is Dr. Leeland, and you will refer to me as Dr. Leeland and nothing else, feel free to call me any of the profanity-riddled names I'm sure you're thinking of in the safety of your own head."

I looked straight into the witch's eyes, and with a deep swing, smacked the stupid glasses right off of her wrinkled face, screaming "HUTTON. IT'S HUTTON. BLAKE HUTTON."

Just kidding. I took my seat.

She was the no-nonsense, old school kind of teacher that still argues taking paddling out of school was the worst thing this country has ever done. So I knew this would be the class where I came in and smiled and sat there pretending to do work with my mouth shut. I was hoping she was the kind of woman who wouldn't bother me as long as I returned the favor.

After class, Mikey came up to me to say sorry but ended up laughing more than apologizing.

"Well, I'm gonna take the blame for what might be the worst first impression you could ever give to your teacher." I told him it was no big deal, but he apologized again and walked me to my third period English class.

My English class was taught by Mr. Brubaker. His classroom was welcoming; various posters of Shakespeare's and other famous classics clung to the walls of his closet shaped classroom. I liked the poster in the corner that read:

"Write good and hard about what hurts."
-Ernest Hemingway

He was very nice to me, and an overwhelming smile crept across his face when I told him I loved English and writing. "You better not just be sucking up," he joked. He was a measly five foot eight but thick and muscular with golden hair. The total opposite of the poster boy English teacher.

Class went by quickly and painlessly. We reviewed *Lord of the Flies*, which I had read twice already, making it the perfect period for me to relax and daydream. I worried about who I would sit with at lunch, but besides that, I wasn't all that worked up.

After English, I found Olivia and she walked me to the counselors to help me schedule the rest of my classes. I had chosen astronomy, a study hall, and two art classes, hoping that since half of the year was already over, this would make the rest very painless.

Next, she walked me to the planetarium, telling me to find her at lunch so I could meet her friends. I spent the remainder of the period in awe at the projections of planets on the top of the dome-shaped planetarium. The teacher, Mr. Trimble was a zany man who was wearing as many colors and patterns on his clothes as he could fit. Yellow stripes with a red and green flowered tie, but yet he seemed like the man that could pull it off. He spiked his hair with enough gel that would only be possible if he was spending half of his yearly salary on hair products.

I left astronomy and followed the flood all the way to the cafeteria… or should I say food court? You could tell half of the schools budget went to the court. There was a rip-off subway in one corner, a burger joint that smelled like actual beef and not pink mystery meat in the other. An untouched salad bar ran through the middle. It reminded me of when I went away to a volleyball camp at Millersville University in 8th grade, and we were practically given the keys to the cafeteria.

I was sadly mistaken when I thought the hallways in between classes were as violent as it got, the food court was an all-out war zone. Turning and contorting my body to get in between everyone was exhausting, and all I managed to land was a yogurt parfait and peanut butter and jelly sandwich, which was pretty much useless once I discovered it was wheat bread.

I had more "get the hell out of the way"s and dirty looks thrown at me in those few minutes than I've probably had in my eighteen years of life. Escaping the foodcourt with only minor sweat stains under my arms and a bruised ego, I saw Olivia waving me down from across the room, and I sped over to her. Not before blindsiding a kid walking from around the other side of a table. Coating him in a fine layer of yogurt parfait.

"Shit, oh my God! I'm so sorry!"

He looked up at me more confused than mad. "Is that how you make friends where you come from?" He was bald. Not a hair on his head. But his defined jaw and crystallized blue eyes evened it out. Of course, the added yogurt helped out too. I was frozen in disbelief; I had just pulled the most embarrassing new girl move in the book. He followed with "Alrighty then, don't worry about the shirt," and on he went. I turned around to find the entire lunchroom, yes the entire lunchroom, zeroed in on me.

I was in a trance from that moment on. I went through my last three periods speaking the least amount possible. A shroud of embarrassment sat heavily on my shoulders.

CHAPTER THREE

I stood in the lot, watching a barrage of cars fly in and out, all full of people trying to get away from this place as fast as possible. At least I fit in in that sense. Tommy Lee whipped up to the curb, and I jumped in.

"So?"

"So what?" I asked.

"Well, I mean, how did it go obviously?"

"I don't know, Dad. I mean I spilled a tray on a bald kid and almost got my first detention, so I would have to say it was a raging success. Can't wait to go back."

"A bald kid?"

"A bald kid, Dad. I figured his day was already going bad when he woke up today and ran out the door without his wig, so I just wanted to see if I could make it any worse."

He just looked at me.

"Well, you know what they say about rock bottom?"

"Just shut up."

He finished anyway, "only up from here." He laughed alone because there was nothing funny about the new girl embarrassing the shit out of herself at a new school, in a new town, in front of all new people. I laid my head against the window and held back tears the whole way home.

"Home sweet home," Tommy Lee said.

Yes, it may have walls and a roof and a door and a great big backyard with a hot tub and a nice pretty fence lining the property and a garage that should have three cars in it, but as we pull in, only two fill it. It might have all of the characteristics of a home, but this is not *my* home. Tommy Lee and I had been here for a little over a week, and boxes still sprung out through the house.

A week is not enough time to move in all of my memories. The kitchen might have new marble countertops, but those aren't the countertops where my yearly birthday cake sat. The new dining room doesn't hold the same smell of candles. The living room couch cushion isn't worn in from where I sat every day after school to watch TV. I try not to dwell on it too much, but I keep it in the back of my head to tread carefully. I'm still walking in foreign land.

Tommy Lee and I walk in through the side door, and he gave a great big "Hello" to see if Miss Josefina was there. A cheery "Hello" was returned in a sweet broken accent.

I told him I was going to chill in my room for a little, and he looked sad. I'm guessing he wanted to spend some quality time watching TV or something, but I'd much rather nap.

My room was still bland with nothing on the walls and there were still bags of clothes everywhere. This depressed me even more. I shrugged off the overbearing stylistic quietness off my room and cocooned myself in my covers. My phone buzzed, and a number flashed at the top of my screen. I recognized the number and instantly felt a pit form at the bottom of my stomach. My mother. I had gotten enough courage to delete her contact, but I wasn't fully ready to block her number. It was somewhat nice to know she still called and wanted to apologize, but she should be directing those phone calls towards Tommy Lee instead.

Roughly two weeks ago, he had stormed into my room.

"Get up, and please put some pants on," he laughed, "You in the mood for a Sunday drive?"

In the midst of drowning in a History paper, I jumped at the offer.

"You still writing that thing?"

The answer was yes, but not because it was hard, but more so because I thought I deserved a ten-minute break every time I successfully wrote a sentence.

"Don't even worry about writing that thing, let's just go have some fun," he coaxed He seemed like he was holding something back, mostly tears, and I could tell something was wrong. My parents had been extraordinarily happy and nice the month leading up to that moment. Not to each other, just to me. We hit the road; stopping at McDonald's to pig out, and drove for about an hour and a half. I didn't question where we were going or why. We always took drives like this, not as many lately, but we always found time for a drive at least once a month. We would drive out and vent about everything that pissed us off; mine usually pertained to boys, while his vents were full of politics, problems at work, or rude stuff my mother had said to him. It was actually a pretty great time.

When I saw we were in Park Pendleton, I was slightly confused. The usual destination was somewhere up the mountain. Park Pendleton had a huge, and I mean huge, mall, so I was praying for a day of shopping. We ended up driving through this really ritzy neighborhood, and he told me all about how he had always wanted to live in a big house with a fence since he was little. Tommy Lee grew up without two nickels to rub together and was often picked on and shunned from friend groups for being the dirtball. He told me football was the only reason people talked to him. We followed this great windy road through the fantastic neighborhood. The road wrapped around the small mountain and leveled out at the top, where the even nicer homes sat.

"Would be something else to grow up in a house like this," he said, as we pulled out front of a gorgeous white house. He was in tears at this point, pulling out a key. My heart sank. I still didn't know what was going on, but I could tell he had just pulled a very stupid Tommy Lee move.

I followed him into the estate, my mind fumbling through all of the possibilities of exactly what the hell is going on. He sat me down on a lonely couch sitting directly in the middle of the bare living room. All I really had to say was 'wow.' The place was beyond gorgeous. White walls and high ceilings. At the time, I had no clue what words were about to come out of his mouth. He put his arm around me and pulled me in close, "Your mother and I need some time away." The words broke both of our hearts. I don't know whether sending or receiving that awful, terrible sentence hurt more. He went to speak again, "I'm going to be sta…" and broke off into immediate weeping. All I did was hug him harder and try to

match his wails, showing him it was okay to cry.
I couldn't even make sense of the situation.
Crying, random couch, nice house, divorce?
My father could probably count on one hand the number of times I had seen him cry. His worn, leathery hands would probably extend a middle finger: for when he watched his team, the Carolina Panthers, get their asses kicked in Super Bowl 50. Second finger would be for my 10th Christmas, when we sat together crying because he couldn't scrape together more than a hundred dollars for gifts. In the grand scheme of things, this didn't change or ruin my life, so no big deal. God forbid I didn't get my Super Deluxe Barbie Playhouse. Final finger would be this moment right here.

So we sat, and we talked. I know it hurt him to tell me just as much, if not more than it did to hear. My mother was having an affair. Some prick receptionist from her law firm. A receptionist. The "hello, what can I do for you" guy. I didn't even think guys were receptionists in the first place, and now one is stealing my mother from us.

It broke my heart to hear him try to force the explanation out through his sobbing breaths. He was hard to understand. Never in my life had I seen my father like this, and it was the most terrible feeling having to just watch him and know there was nothing I could do.

My mother had been staying extra late at the office lately. It made so much sense; I couldn't believe what I was hearing. There's no way. I rejected this. My mother would never do that. To me, my father is the best man in the world. He worked his ass off to give us everything.

He wiped the snot and tears from his face and wrapped his arms around me. His arms were very tense. There was no sign of him letting go, so we just sat there and talked while hugging.

"Where does this house fall into things?" I asked.

"I, uh, we decided, well," he could barely get his words out. "Your mother is going to keep the old house."

He had found out about her cheating when she said she was going to stay extra late to work on a case. He wanted to drop by and bring her dinner. When he pulled up to the office, though, not a car in sight. To make it worse, while he's calling her trying to find out where she is, he passes her car on the way back to the house. He passes her car... in the guy's driveway... four blocks from our house. Jesus, I mean you might as well just bring the guy over for dinner.

They talked about it for a while, but he said they never made any progress; she wanted to keep seeing the guy. He liquidated his entire stock portfolio to buy his dream house here in Park Pendleton because his best friend, Kenny, from high school lives here. Which makes sense I guess, but I mean buying a borderline mansion an hour and a half away from your family to hang out and drink beers with your best friend smells an awful lot like a midlife crisis.

    Then he gave me the option: I could stay with my mother or move here, to Park Pendleton.

CHAPTER FOUR

Coddled in my blankets, I consider if it's actually worth it to ever get out of bed, like ever again. I would've honestly liked to hear a real argument as to why anyone should ever leave their bed. Some would say to work, to that I say hell no. I could make more than enough money selling pictures of my feet to old men over the internet, or when business is slow, I could do like a cam show for a quick buck. That gives me a nice monthly budget to take care of pizza and Chinese delivery. The issue of proper hygiene is little more than a speed bump in my plan. Thirty dollars for a bulk delivery of adult diapers from Amazon Prime to take care of my restroom needs. I think I could really pull this off. Just as I'm logging on to make an account on *sellyourfeet.com* my phone starts ringing again. Olivia.

I answer confused. She answered in her excited sweet tone.

"Blake Blake Blake, what is going on at the Huston household right now?"

I consider trying to get her to buy in on my soon to be foot porn empire but settle with a much more simple "nothing really, why?"

"Well if you're not doing anything, you could come to the mall, I'll introduce you to a couple of my friends. You could probably stay over tonight, too, if you want," she says.

A chance to make some actual friends.

"Ah what the hell, you're gonna have to pick me up though."

"Awesome," she says, "send me your location; I'll be there in a little." Click.

Olivia had talked to me at lunch a little, and I met a couple of her friends, but I didn't know she liked me enough to actually want to be seen with me outside of school. I was completely prepared to just become school friends with a couple of people to make my daily seven-hour sentence a bit less lonely, but I had no intention of making new friends here.

Coincidentally, as I'm trying to pick out a semi-cute outfit to not embarrass myself in front of Olivia and her friends, one of my friends from Richmont Caramel texted me to see if I was home with my mom for the weekend. Funny. I replied with "lol" to which she replied with "how's the new school," to which I then replied "steal me back, please."

I threw on a pair of ripped jeans and dug through my bags to find a shirt. My phone lit up. "Here." On my way out, I went down to the basement to Tommy Lee's man cave where he was sitting in his old musty leather recliner. The same one he's had since I was born.

"Where you going, kiddo?"

"I'm gonna head to the mall with a couple girls," I told him.

"Woah, I get it, you only come see me when you need cash," he chuckled. I didn't even ask, but he handed me a hundred and forty in twenties and fives.

"Are you sure?" I asked.

"Of course, get some new clothes or something, new school, new you, right?"

"Thanks." I ask him if he's going out with his friends tonight and he just nods no, "Just gonna stay in and watch a movie or something."

I told him I loved him and that I would text him to check in later. On my way out he stopped me,

"Hey, I told you."

"Told me what?" I ask.

"You'd make friends in no time, go have fun, I love you."

I hopped into Olivia's car. It's about as clean as you would expect from a teenager. Cheap lemon air fresheners contaminated the air. Two other girls just like her sat in the back seat. They're dressed like her, except a bit more hipster/hippie, even the same hair styles.

"Ello mate," Olivia greeted me with a well-practiced British accent.

Her friends did this weird thing where they go into hour long spurts of speaking in British accents. I chose not to partake in this. I turned around to the girls in the back. One of the girls is black with a big ring septum piercing through her nose that makes her look like she was trying awfully hard to pass as a bull instead of young, teenage hipster.

"Hey, Blake!" the girls squealed. I had met them earlier at lunch, but couldn't remember either of their names. I made a mental note to really listen for their names because half of the time they just refer to each other as "bitch" or "girl." There was little room for conversation on the way, too busy screaming song lyrics like we were performing them ourselves.

We pulled up to the mall, and I did my best to scrape my jaw off the seat and reattach it to my mouth. The mall from Richmont was little more than a movie theater with a bookstore and two clothes stores attached. The Park Pendleton City Mall's parking garage was about the same size as the mall itself. On the inside, escalators and bridges connected to different floors and stores. Magnificent statues and pieces of local made art were placed throughout. A playground lay in the very center. It was a dream. The architects were obviously half baked and more than inspired by Willy Wonka's chocolate factory when they drew this bad boy up. My neck turned side to side, brand name stores lined the walls as far as the eyes could see. As far as I was concerned, this was my new home.

"Where do we even start in this place?" I asked.
They just laughed.
The bull girl said she was going to stop downstairs to grab some cigarettes and then meet up with us. Just like that we were off into the land of expensive shirts made by young children in China and indulging in everything else that capitalism and consumerism had to offer. I knew how to make my money work for me, and I had no doubt I was walking out of there with bags upon bags. We started at one end and worked our way to the other. The Bull met up with us in Victoria's Secret just in time for their seven for twenty nine dollar sale.
I was buying stuff here and there. The girls were really cool and welcoming to me. The Bull turned out to be quite a softy, despite her looks.

She snuck out from the dressing room in Victoria's Secret, grabbed us, took the bra from my hand and lowly whispered it was time to go. Once we were out of the store, I asked why and they just seemed to chuckle at me.

"You mean you've been paying for your stuff the whole time?" said the other girl who wasn't the Bull, but I still hadn't picked up her name.

"Well, I mean, I'm not a thief."

She raised an eyebrow, I think I offended her, but I mean I'm not a thief. Tommy Lee would kick my ass if I stole. I would kick my ass if I stole. I didn't want to piss them off, though. I was just getting over being nervous in front of them, and they were starting to open up to me.

"But, to each his own," I said quickly in an effort to save myself.

We continued on with our glorious spree, until I realized I had less than ten dollars left.

Olivia started, "We can leave whenever you want. We were just gonna go back to my place and just watch movies tonight or do whatever."

I was having fun though and I still hadn't seen the entire mall, so I said we can keep going; I still wanted to get some food.

"I'll take you to the food court! You girls go commit all the crimes you want, and we'll meet up at the makeup corner in fifteen," Olivia offered.

"The. The. The what?" I asked.

"We saved the best for last! At the other end, there's a whole row of makeup stores with every color of everything you'd ever want. Thank us later," Olivia said.

"Dammit. You guys should have told me earlier. I spent like all of my money," I admitted.

The Bull butted in, "Don't worry, girl, we got you. This is why it's nice to know a thief or two."

The Bull and the other girl, whose name I think was Sammy, but I wasn't sure enough to say it yet, took off in the other direction while we headed straight through the heart of retail row to the food court.

The food court, if you haven't guessed, was just as immaculate as the rest of the mall. It was a cultural melting pot. Thai food in the corner, subs over here, burgers here, authentic Italian pizza here, a seafood bar on this end. I was in love. Olivia wasn't hungry so she just stood in line with me while I drooled over the options.

"It's okay to be overwhelmed. Imagine the first time I came in here when I was six; the place was pretty much like a city to me." I pictured a young Olivia, still in her striped cropped shirt and ripped mom jeans, running through the mall in awe like she was in time square. I couldn't help but think that was exactly what I looked like.

We stood in line to get cheesesteaks behind the Thai restaurant workers. I guess they would probably hate Thai food by now.
While I was listening in on their Thai conversation that I had no hopes of understanding, Olivia grabbed my arm lightly, "It's alright, I don't like stealing either."

"Don't take this the wrong way, but why do you hang out with them then? If you get caught with them I'm pretty sure you go down with them. It's like guilty by association, isn't it?"

She laughed a little, "No, it's alright. It's just... they're honestly great friends. They've been with me through a lot of shit, so I mean when you find people who really care about you, you pick your battles, ya know? You don't throw away people like them; they're hard to come by. I'm not gonna just decide our friendship isn't worth anything because they don't like to pay for makeup and bras."
I told her I guess that made sense.
I was really starting to like Olivia Books.

She started again, "Plus, Sandra practically let me live with her when my mom kicked me out."
Sandra. That was the other girl's name.

"Kicked you out?" I asked.

"Yeah, not a good situation. We're okay now...it was just a falling out."

I got my cheesesteak, and we made our way to the makeup corner of the mall. The girls were waiting there with their bags full of clothes and makeup and lack of morals.
It. Was. Beautiful.
While I was busy wiping my tears on my sleeve, the girls took off into Sephora. They would watch to see what I picked up, and then grab it after I walked away. It was kind of a compliment, unless they just genuinely enjoyed stealing, it meant they liked me enough to commit a misdemeanor.

"Hey, Olivia! What are you guys doing here?" a voice called out from behind one of the racks. Out walked Kennedy D'Angelo, the IT girl at Park Pendleton. She and Olivia, despite being in two totally different friend groups, were always good friends since middle school. She had long, gorgeous, dark hair done into a ponytail that ran down the back of her sun kissed skin. I was kind of fangirling over her, I'm not going to lie.

While Olivia and she talked, the Bull and the other girl whose name I had already forgotten continued on their spree. Then, like something out of a movie, the Bull gave girl two a nod. What happened next could only have been executed as well as it did by the sheer abundance of practice and some great acting skills.
Girl two walked right in front of the sole cashier and proceeded to faceplant while knocking over a small display. The Bull moved like a phantom,

collecting everything else she had been eyeing up.
She swooped behind me, girl two jumped up off
the floor and apologized to the cashier whose day
just got a lot worse, and then we left.
Kennedy walked out with us giggling because she
knew what was going on.
She looked at me, "you're the new girl right?"
I nodded yes.

"Well did you get invited to Dizzy's
party?"
Then I nodded no.

"Well let's do something about that," she
said.

"What kind of party?" I asked, because
the only parties I've been to were birthday
parties, which definitely weren't the same kind of
parties these guys liked.

"Oh please," She said, "you'll have fun,
I'll introduce you to everyone and you can get a
proper Park Pendleton welcome."
Olivia and the girls looked at me, "up to you,"
they said. Olivia told me not to worry if I didn't
feel comfortable.

"Don't judge me," I said "but I've never
actually been to a party"
Kennedy answered quickly, "It's settled then, you
HAVE to go, how else are you gonna meet
everyone."
I gave in, "But," I said, "I'm not drinking
tonight." I told them it's because I had stuff to do

with Tommy Lee in the morning. They just smirked at each other and Kennedy gave me a "whatever you say." The truth was though I've tried one sip of alcohol in my life. Back when I was nine or ten, Tommy Lee let me take a sip out of his beer, and in return, I spit it in his face. I had no understanding as to how anyone could drink that shit.

Olivia asked, "Dizzy's house, right?"

"Yup, you can come whenever after ten, but that's what time I'll be getting there," Kennedy answered.

"Alright, mates, it's settled," Olivia said after.

This wasn't exactly the worst thing that could happen. I needed to make friends with the popular kids anyways. Kennedy was everything I wanted to be at Richmont and she's everything I could be now that I have a fresh start.

The plan was separated into four easy parts.

Get Tommy Lees permission (easiest part)
Meet cute boys (hardest part)
Don't get drunk (very do-able)
Get closer with everyone and make a name for myself other than "new girl.'"

I called Tommy Lee to ask about staying at Liv's. He gave me a, "no I don't care, just text me when you get home kiddo. Have fun, but not too much fun." as the go ahead. I could picture it in my head, his still reclined in his chair, Sports Center on, Cheetos crumbs everywhere, he probably had to lick his fingers clean before answering the phone. I almost felt a little guilty about the whole thing. He had no idea what I was about to go do or where. Honestly, I had no idea either. Park Pendleton was more than a new beginning; it was time for me to expand. I'm tired of being the girl who goes home and gets her work done and goes to bed. I'm tired of ordering takeout Friday night with Tommy Lee being the most fun thing I do all week.

Going to the party is starting to make me sweat a little, I'm just nervous about meeting everyone; I can see it all play out now.

I walk in with Olivia and her friends

Whole party: HEY GUYS COME PAR…. wait… who the hell is she with?

Me: Hi my name is Bla-

Whole party: THAT'S THE NEW GIRL

queue everybody laughing hysterically at the new girl

Random kid in the back: SHE THREW HER FOOD ON THE BALD KID

Other random kid: WHY YOU GOTTA MESS WITH THE BALD KID

Olivia and her friends: Sorry you're gonna have to walk home, we can't be seen with you.

whole party boos me as I leave crying
Dramatic? Maybe. A possibility of happening? Likely. I couldn't stop thinking about the kid from lunch. So stupid. So so stupid. Just a second's difference and I could have walked right around him, no scene, no being stared at, no ruining a bald kid's day. The rumors going around are probably awful. Oh God, the rumors. Talk spread fast at my old school, but it was small and everybody knew everybody and their mother. And their mother's mother. And their mother's mothers son's cousin, who was probably their cousin too. Maybe since this school was big enough to swallow my school and still have room for seconds, word would spread slower. I've seen those halls, and all the kids it holds. No way that story would have ended up in everyone's ear. But then again, more kids mean more mouths. I had reached full sweat, soaking right through my shirt. This was going to spread like a wildfire.
We were in Liv's car headed through downtown; I reach up through the back seat and turn the music down.
Three mouths mutter "Aye what the hell, mate?" in perfect unison.

"The bald boy"

"The one you covered in yogurt?" asked the Bull.

"Yes, the one wearing my designer parfait, who is he?" I asked

"Oh his names Atlas," Olivia answered, "he's like really nice I think, but I don't know a thing about him. He's not like a weirdo or anything, though."

Girl two interjected, "He's really nice; he helps me in my engineering class. I don't mind sitting back and watching those hands write my work, gives me time to wonder what else those hands do."

"Stop it, you nasty ass," Olivia interjected.

"Don't even try to say that boy ain't fine, hair or no hair," the Bull added. I asked why he was bald.

"Personal choice," Liv answered.

The Bull laughed, "Bullshit, nobody chooses to be bald. My money's on cancer or lice."

"Alopecia areata," Girl two said, "it's a disease that attacks your hair follicles."

"Oh, did he tell you that?" I asked.

"No, I found it on Google." Her ability to pronounce the name was reason enough for me to take her word.

"Either way, do you think like people are talking about it?" I asked, not sure if I wanted the real answer.

Olivia giggled, "I don't think anyone cares, it would be different if you threw it on Dizzy or one of the football players."

I sighed in relief.

"Good," I said, reaching up to crank the music back to its distortedly loud state. We drove through downtown; they showed me some of the food spots and small boutiques, just trying to kill time before the party. We drove out from under a bridge littered with tipis and makeshift plywood huts, occupied by some unfortunate souls. Coming out from the bridge, I ran my eyes up the seemingly endless floors to the Park Pendleton Area Hospital. Everything in this city was bigger and better. The sleek modern hospital gave off the impression of a place where people would voluntarily pay to stay a couple nights.

We finished our wonderfully British commentated tour and sped off to Dizzy's house, which lay back up in the southern hills of Park Pendleton. The girls explained to me how every other week the football players or cheerleaders are chosen to host a party. Apparently, they have a giant spin wheel with everyone's names on it to select. Dizzy was known to throw absolute bangers.

We drove up through the South Hills, leaving me in utter awe. I was having a tough time comprehending the house, and imagining how many zeros and commas were included in the price of them. The hills were where most of the popular kids lived, and I concluded that it was no coincidence. The houses were immaculate; they looked handcrafted by the angel architects themselves responsible for the golden streets of heaven. And here I was, driving right through them. I was soaking it in; this was where I wanted to be. I was also somewhat humbled thinking I was living in the nicest neighborhood. These estates made mine look like a groundskeeper's shack.

Dizzy's house was monstrous. I heard people at school call him the King of Park Pendleton, and that's exactly who this house was fit for. He sat on a throne of money, athletic scholarships, and designer clothes. From what I saw today, it was damn near impossible to walk through the halls without his name being brought up. Whether it was about how hot he was or how much of a dick he was, there was no denying his name was everywhere.

Cars lined every road for blocks up to his house. I thought we were trying to get there early but we couldn't go a block without Liv lowering her window to talk to people from school on their way up to his house. We parked and began the hike up to Dizzy's.

The girls were excited, saying that we got a good parking spot. I asked them who would be here.

"You don't even have to be invited, if you're not popular you can still come, but you just have to bring your own alcohol," Liv informed me.

"So his parents just let him do this?" I asked.

"His parents are friends with the other snobs' parents, they go out of town for the weekend together and then the snobs throw parties while they're gone. It's $5 to drink, and then they use some of that to pay people to clean up the next day," Liv said back. The snobs were beginning to sound more like an exclusive club than a group of teenagers. I wanted in.

"And what about the leftover cash?"

"They use it to fund the next party," she said laughing.

"I'm nervous, I don't know a soul." This was a slight understatement. My new girl nightmares were manifesting in every inch of my head. I had continent-sized pit stains forming under both arms, growing rapidly as if the tectonic plates of my armpits were forming the second Pangea.

"Don't be," the Bull told me. "Just wait you're gonna love it; you'll meet people once we get a little liquid courage in you."

"Yeah funny," I told her as we started up the winding driveway to his castle.
Rap music blasted from inside the house. It was loud enough to have a separate party a block away. Olivia yelled up to her friend hanging out the third story window. He had what I thought was a cigarette in his mouth, with smoke rolling

out from behind him. This shit was intimidating. The whole front yard reeked like skunk.

I asked them if they smelled it, and they laughed hard at me.

"Honey that ain't no skunk," the bull laughed.

"Ooh girl I am excited!" Girl two squealed.

"Great. Tommy will rip every strand of hair from my head if I even go near marijuana."

The Bull stopped me, "Just say weed, and you'll be fine, just relax."

We knocked on the front door, and a towering black kid wearing his Park Pendleton football jersey opened up, taking us into a small entryway room with another door into the house. The vibrations from the music were running up my leg.

"Whatsup guys, you drinking?" he asked.

"Duhh, why else would we be here?" Girl two said laughing.

He looked at me, "new girl right?"

I answered yes.

"You're free," he said, stamping my hand with an orange bingo dauber.

"Thanks, Deshawn, what a sweetheart," the Bull said. He smiled at her.
The other girls handed over their money and got stamped. Another knock came from the first door.

He told us we were good and opened the door up to the house, then closed it behind us and went to let the next person in.

The music was loud to the point it almost hurt. The entryway dumped you into a lobby-like room. Two staircases on opposite sides up the room joined together on a top balcony, taking you up to the second floor. People were dancing, spilling their drinks on each other without a single care. There were speakers in the main room. As we walked through, I didn't get any of the dirty confused stares I thought I would.

A scrawny kid, no taller than me, ran up to Liv and gave her a hug. He was wearing an extravagant lampshade on his head, with eyes and a mouth hole cut out.

"Yo, Lampshade DeLoache! I thought you were grounded from last week?" Liv screamed so he could hear her over the music.

"They can't keep me locked up, you should know that by now! Twenty-seven straight appearances and counting! You gotta see the collection," he yelled back. He pulled out two small plastic sauce containers from his pockets.

"Jell-O anybody?"

"Um yes, please," Liv answered.

He handed her the small containers. Liv kept one and passed the other to me.

"Jell-O I asked?

"Yeah, just eat it, trust me."

I took the cap off while they sat there watching me like I was some animal in a science experiment.

"I've had Jell-O before guys."

I tried to squeeze the Jell-O out into my mouth and ended up crushing it up along with the container.

"Jesus we should've known better," Liv said laughing, "Just scoop the rest out."

I choked the Jell-O down. "What the hell is this?" It left a trail of burning and bitterness down my throat.

The girls laughed hard together at me, leaving me confused on what was going on.

"Congrats, mate! You just slugged down your first Jell-O shot."

Before I could yell at them they laughed some more, "Relax, mate, Sandra's driving us home."

"She better," I answered. "Seriously. How is that enjoyable anyway? I just ate solid nail polish."

Somebody called out at Lampshade from the hall underneath the two joining staircases, and he took off, bobbing in and out of dancing groups of people, his hand holding onto the lampshade so nobody could snatch it.

"Care to explain?" I asked.

"His name's Kevin Deloache, crazy ass kid. He has a tradition of going to every single party and stealing a lampshade to wear around that night. The kid's got an entire shrine of them in his closet. It's to the point where they just buy him one and have it ready for him so they don't have to try and replace whichever one he takes the next day."

"What the hell is wrong with the people at this school?"

"C'mon, we're wasting time, we should be chugging right now," Liv followed up.
They grabbed my hand and pulled me back the hall. It dropped us right in the middle of the kitchen. Speakers hung from all corners of the room, the island was taped off with caution tape around it, and bottles of every color lined the island. A tall kid wearing a beanie with headphones over the top and a yellow hoodie stood behind the island next to a bunch of music equipment, taking song requests and swapping out to pour everybody drinks. There was a 3-foot pyramid of the Jell-O cup containers sitting on the counter behind him with an "uno dolla" sign next to the monument.
We continued through every room of the house, I followed Liv and her friends as they tried to find others they knew and introduce me. After meeting her whole band of Drama club friends, I asked her to maybe set her sights on introducing me to boys of a 7/10 grade or higher.

We funneled through the other rooms out onto the back porch. It was immaculate. The patio beneath my feet shook to the bass drops from the speakers overhead. Every second I looked out over his backyard, my heart raced faster. This is what I've been missing out on. Christmas lights and toilet paper lined the trees throughout the yard. The yard itself went on back as far as you could see until the light dimmed out, leaving the yelling, music, and the whizzing around of phone screens as a testament of the partiers back there.
People crowded around the pool, lights strobed behind people as guys tackled each other into the water, and girls stripped off all but their underwear to jump in after them. I'd place a solid bet that the pool consisted of more alcohol than water at this point.

"Didn't you say we got here early?" I asked Liv.

"We did, mate."

I followed them down the steps off the patio and around the back corner of the pool where a circle formed out of the mass of dancers. We push our way to the front as cheap beer from careless people rained down on us. There was no way I could wear this home tomorrow. Liv and the Bull plowed through up to the front. Somebody tapped my shoulder and handed me their unfinished cup. Kennedy was standing, barely, with a group of other girls next to a few football players. In front of them lay three kegs in a triangle.

"You guys came!" Kennedy squealed, wobbling over to us. She hugged us one by one. "I'm so excited you guys came." She reeked. "Ooh, Blake let me introduce you to my friends." She pulled me over to the group she came from. She seemed just like a little ball of drunken energy. She seemed fun. She seemed like the exact opposite of me for the last eighteen years. Mikey P was in the group, he said hi to me, and then Kennedy introduced me to everyone else. I was seriously worried about her. She was a time bomb full of vomit and alcohol and God knows what else, about to blow any second

"This is King Dizzy," she tugged on his shirt to get his attention. "This is Blake, the one I was telling you about."

What could she have told him about me? He turned around, almost blinding me with the shine from his teeth. He. Was. Beautiful. His skin was sweet milk chocolate, absolutely flawless, not a scar, mark or pimple.

"Whatup, new girl, Blake right?" smiling as he talked, his teeth were the textbook definition of perfect. The dimples on the corner of his smile fried my brain. I had no clue how to even move my mouth, or what to say back if I could. I thought quickly.

"Uh, cool party."

He cocked his head, running a hand through his hair, "Thanks," he chuckled, "but it is Blake, right?"

"Oh. Yeah."

"Cool," he said, putting his arm around me.

"Well you know, we have to give you a correct Park Pendleton welcome. We need to show you what we're about here. He was leaning in so close to me, the ice from his breathe chilled my face, and the jean jacket he was wearing filled the boundaries around him with an aroma, unlike anything I've ever smelled before. It smelled cool if that makes any sense.

"Well, what would that be?" I said giggling.

He let go of me and jumped up onto the kegs.

"Attentiioonn," he screamed out. "Kegggg chuugggggg!"

The party roared in a glass shattering wail that probably woke Tommy Lee up.

The crowd turned in uniform towards the keg. The music switched to a hard rap song.

"Wha...what's in there?" I asked Dizzy.

"Don't worry about that, you got this."

I definitely did not have this.

I can't even chug a Coke without choking it up and burping for the next five minutes. But everybody's eyes were on me. This was my chance to let everyone know who I was. Dizzy started a Blake chant, and soon my name was a sound wave of encouragement. No time to bitch out.

"Alright," I said still on the edge about it.

"You wanna go upside down?" Mikey asked me.

"Upside down? Easy there, tiger, let's take baby steps."

"Ight, well get down on ya knees then," Dizzy butted in.

My name was getting louder and louder.

I put my cup down and they put the pump in my mouth, beer rushed down my throat. I was experiencing a different kind of burning. My eyes teared up, and I started choking on it, but they wouldn't shut it off. I was just funneling it down, trying to breathe in through my nose.

"You're at ten! Keep going!" Dizzy screamed in my ear.

"Blake. Blake. Blake." It kept getting louder, and my throat kept burning more. The beer was freezing.

I couldn't take it anymore, the pump shot out my mouth with beer and fizz following it.

"Seventeen, not bad," Dizzy announced.

The yard erupted.

"Yes, Blake! Yes, that's my bitch!" Liv screamed, coming to hug me.

I was still coughing when Kennedy jumped in front of Liv and grabbed me, directing me over to her friends.

"Not bad, new girl," Dizzy said as he grabbed my legs and threw me up in the air. The crowd collapsed underneath me, hands up and down my back, even one on my butt getting a cheap grab.

The name chants got even louder. Girls squealing and guys whistling at me. The song changed, and I came down. The DJ kid had set up a second table on the porch pouring cups and shots, people were grabbing as many as they could and passing them out through the yard. Dizzy and Mikey grabbed me and took me towards the top of the yard. Handing me cups, "Here, drink this one next," I was downing every cup they gave me. An awful scowl came across my face, each shot was getting harder.

After a while, they left to go dancing, and I linked back up with Olivia and the other girls.

"That was epiccc!" Liv screamed.

"I think I'm gonna die. Either that or I'm just gonna kill myself."

"I think that's like the same thing, Blake."

"I told you not to let me drink!"

"Yeah, but it was so cool."

"You think it was cool?"

"Um, yeah," the other girl popped in with approval.

"You think Dizzy and Kennedy thought so too?" I asked.

"Um, probably. Why?"

I changed the subject back, "Seriously though, I smell terrible. I can't go home like this."

"Just change into some of the clothes you bought earlier; they're in my car still."

The Bull interjected, "How about we deal with this later and worry more about dancing and getting smashed. Blake looks set, but I've only had one drink."

"Yeah, Blake is set," I said.

We started dancing into the crowd, with each new song we drove deeper into the mosh pit. Being drunk was just some imaginary realm I had heard about up to that point. I could barely keep myself up and even worse, keep the liquor down. Eventually, I involuntarily danced myself over by the pool. The pool was the centerpiece of the party, pulling it all together. Some kids were in the water playing chicken, someone else was handing their shoe over to their friend, barely getting it to them before they threw up. One girl was topless on the diving board, jumping up and down as a crowd around her cheered and shouted different tricks for her to do. Occasionally you would get a glimpse of Kennedy weaving in and out of groups of guys, stealing a sip of their drinks and leaving them a kiss as payment. I didn't even know I could dance until now, but I was ripping the party up. I had also never grinded on anyone before, but that night was a night of firsts. The dancing was careless, no regards were taken for anyone around you, my shoes were completely destroyed, most likely along with my liver. Dizzy worked his way over to me. Not a word was spoken, he just grabbed me and pulled me against him.

I was hoping to pick up some of his cologne to give me a reason to never wash this shirt. He pulled me closer and closer until we were almost sharing the same breath. He put his lips against my skin and laced kisses up my neck. My body was tingling. He worked his way to my lips and then over to my ear.

"You know there's a party inside, too?"

"It's fun out here though," I answered.

"We could come back out after."

"Who's inside? Just bring them out here," I said giggling, "The more the merrier."

"Let's throw our own party. Lemme show you my room."

My eyes widened. I didn't know what to say. He grabbed my wrist. "Come on, let's go. I'll show you the whole house."

I couldn't say no. I was frozen again.

Somebody from behind me stopped Dizzy. "Not cool, man. Don't do that."

"Mind ya business, bro. You're at my crib, remember."

"You heard me, not cool."

"Yeah whatever," Dizzy answered back, grabbing me, kissing me, and pulling away to stare at whoever was behind me. Then, he was swallowed up in the sea of moving colors and blobs. I was getting wobbly. I turned around to see who had stopped him, but I was met by the back of another person's head.

I danced my way over to the edge of the pool, where the pit of students was almost falling into. The heads around me bobbing to the song was hypnotizing; the screaming was started to fade. As I stepped along the edge of the pool, I felt myself losing control. I started tipping over. A hand grabbed the back of my shirt, pulling me back up. He spun me around, "You alright there?" The strobe lights shined off his head. Bald. I was looking at the bald kid I dumped my tray on.

"My hero!" I said throwing my arms around him. I put my hand on his head. "I've never felt a bald guy."

"We seem to be a rare breed this early in life."

I laughed.

"You're funny."

"And you're wasted. You were about to take a swim fully clothed."

I rubbed my hand on his head and down his jaw, it was strong.

"You're uh... um, what's the...handsome, you're very handsome," I said laughing.

"Thank ya, madam. I think you should come with me," he took my hand, gently.

"No, I don't want to go upstairs."

"Relax, you're not talking to Dizzy."

He walked me inside, it was cleared out, for the most part, everyone went outside where the real party was. He handed me a bottle of water. I took a good look at him.

"You are a lot better looking without yogurt on your face.

"I wish you didn't have to ruin my favorite shirt to find that out, but thanks. Here, sit down," he said, ushering me onto the sofa in the living room. "I'll be back in a little bit to check on you."

"No don't go. I wanna go party; I wanna dance, let's dance. Or we could take shots."

"I really don't think you need any more shots. Like for the rest of your life."

"C'mon take me out with you. Don't leave," I begged.

He sat down next to me. "You want me to go find any of your friends for you?"

"No, I just wanna dance. The parties here are insane. It's like something out of *The Great Gatsby*."

"Gatsby? You like *The Great Gatsby*?"
He looked at me wide-eyed with a smile that could melt even the coldest of hearts.
Before I could answer, he was off the chair. "Seriously, just relax for a little bit. You're like turning green. I will be back in a bit." And out of the room he went.
I sat on the couch rolling my head back and forth; the room was spinning. I could feel the puke at the bottom of my throat. My mouth had swapped out with a Saint Bernard's, and I was salivating a lot. My eyes faded out. I couldn't see, but I could still hear what was going around me. I lay there for what was probably a few minutes, drifting off.
"COPS!"
"Cops! There are cops!" it relayed through the yard and up throughout the house.
I was too tired to move.
I could hear everyone running through the house, commotion, screaming, knocking stuff over, somebody shook me.
"Hey! Get up there are cops!"
I heard the sirens.
I felt a firm hand on me.
"C'mon, you beautiful little fool."

CHAPTER FIVE

I woke up to Cimmerian shade surrounding me. I could barely see my hands waving in front of my face. I felt around, my hands grazed over the cracked leather seats I was laying on. I was in a car, the back seat of one. The windows of the car gave way to the surrounding obsidian. It was like black paper was placed over the windows. There was a wool blanket covering me; I pulled it off and felt around for my phone. It was lying on the floor next to a small wastebasket. The time read 12:37 pm. I shined the flashlight through the seats to find a mustang insignia center of the steering wheel. But this wasn't my mustang, the interior was different, this one far older. My clothes. Where were they? No longer in my outfit from last night, I was wearing grey Nike sweatpants and an old black "RJ's Roofing Needs" hoodie. I was panicked. Who did I go home with? Did... did somebody take advantage of me? I looked into my pants, my underwear were still on. But whose car was I in? I shined the light out of the windows to reveal workbenches and toolsets, cabinets and a rack of old basketballs against the walls around me. Whose garage was I in? My breathing picked up. Was I kidnapped? I climbed up over the center console and unlocked the doors, spilling out onto the cement garage floor. Before me sat a gorgeous ice-white mustang, old but well kept. My head was pounding, and the longer I stood up the sicker I felt. My mouth was bitter and reeked of puke.

I walked around the car with my flashlight, checking out the tool boxes and cabinets. A door behind me opened them closed; only letting a strand of clairvoyance grace the garage.

"Rise and shine." The familiar voice called lightly.

"WHO ARE YOU?" I shouted.

"WHERE AM I?"

My screaming only worsened my headache.

"Shhhh be quiet, the hell is wrong with you my dad's outside," the voice reprimanded me.

With the flip of a switch, the garage was lit up. The bald boy stood in front of the door. Relief rolled over me, releasing the tension in my muscles and the idea that I was about to be the victim of some deranged ax murderer, only to be seen one more time when my body would be discovered along a highway or by some hunter, rotting away in the woods. The worries of manslaughter were put to rest, but the situation was still clear, I had been kidnapped by an inexplicably bald teenager.

"I hope the slumber in my stallion wasn't too uncomfortable, but you were out cold so I figured it didn't matter much to you."

I had a list of questions forming in my head; the first one to ring from my mouth could've been worded a little better.

"You better not have touched me or messed with me or anything while I slept. You'll be sorry, you can bet on that."

His brow raised and his eyes widened.

"Hmm, you save a girl from drowning in her own puke, you let her dorm in your restored 66' Mustang, you dress her in your finest of ninth grade garments, and in return, you are accused of rape. Beautiful. Now, who said chivalry was dead?"

"What even happened last night?" I asked him.

"Here, let's go on a drive and we can talk about everything; you look like you need some food."

"I could use some aspirin too… if you're offering."

"Would you like some aspirin?" he asked laughing.

"I would, please."

"Alright, I just threw your clothes in my washer so we can go grab some food and come back in an hour to get them if that's alright with you?"

I nodded then he took off inside to grab his keys and my aspirin.

I sunk into the front seat of his Mustang, the comfiest leather seats I've ever seen in a car. I'm sure Tommy Lee would rather watch football for hours in his front seat over that worn Laz-Y-Boy recliner he lives in. He returned with three red pills and a bottle of water.

"Are you sure these are safe? I mean technically you did just kidnap me, these could be roofies for all I know."

"I guess you'll just have to trust that I'm not using your hangover as a way to drug you and execute my master plan.

I looked at him. He was smiling brilliantly.

"I guess I'll take my chances," I said.

I liked the way he spoke.

He opened the garage, the rays of light illuminated the garage, shining off the frosty white hood of the car. He told me to duck down and I did, pulling out of the garage and down the driveway he waved to his dad who was mowing the lawn, I could tell from the obvious sounds of the mower. He told me it was alright to sit up and as I did, the light pierced my eyes, radiating through the back of my skull.

"I feel like shit," I told him.

"That's probably an understatement, where are we going?" he asked.

"I don't know, something cheap, quantity over quality right now."

"I like the way you think." He added. We drove for a while through town, talking small conversation until we pulled up to a Burger King across from the colossal hospital complex. He ordered me nuggets and fries. He spoke so politely to the drive-through worker, asking her about her day, he even made her laugh, and then left her a tip before we drove away. I didn't know if he was putting on a show for me or what. I couldn't understand how someone spoke with such a warm tone and meant it. It seemed fake. Tommy Lee always told me if it's too good to be true then it probably is, and he was the prime example of such saying. He still hadn't explained anything from last night. It was hard to down the nuggets but I did so out of guilt that he paid. My stomach was churning; my eyes felt heavy in my head, the thought of alcohol was enough to make me gag. He told me I would feel better eventually and pulled over along the side of the road.

"What are you doing?" I asked as he reached over me and got into his glove compartment, pulling out a small canister of Tiger Balm.

"Rub it on your temples and the back of your neck, stuff is magic."

He was right, it didn't take long for me to feel like my eyes were burning out of my head, but my headache was near gone. He drove towards the outskirts of town where abandoned graffitied factories and strips of buildings with plywood in the windows were at every corner. I was wondering where we were going, my earlier fears of being kidnapped by an ax murderer were still on the table, but I didn't question him. We pulled across a railroad track and followed down a road parallel with the woods to our left, ten continued until we came to a small turnoff that was very missable if you weren't expecting it. The road ahead it weaved through the woods and up the mountain. It was just wide enough to fit one car. The woods around it were undisturbed, still untouched from the city of steel and lights from across the tracks. We followed the road for a few minutes, weaving around sharp turns where the trees had replaced the massive buildings of Park Pendleton in towering over us. It was like God's finger lowered from the sky to draw us our own path up to the most beautiful view. At the top of a mountain was a small cul de sac, with trees surrounding it except for the front, where the view opened up out over the city. I hadn't realized until now how beautiful the day was; my lingering hangover couldn't stop me from taking in this view. The isolated cul de sac sat high up, overlooking the grand valley city of Park Pendleton. The towering hospital cast a shadow that swallowed the now pea sized burger king we just left. The valley beyond was breathtaking, stretching far to the east and west, hotels and agencies littered the city. Shopping plazas circled the mega-mall, fermenting the air with the smell of money. The sun rolled down over the mountain across the valley, blanketing the southern hills where Dizzy's castle laid with Kennedy and Mikey P's houses. Seeing their estates poked a feeling of desire and hunger inside me. I should be living in one of those castles. Royalty, that was the Southern Hills, that's where I belonged. I wasn't upset at the house that Tommy Lee bought for us. Well, more or less he bought it for himself, he was going to live there whether I came or not. I couldn't help the feeling that if he had bought us a house in the South Hills, I would have such a better chance at being friends with Kennedy and Dizzy. I really really liked Olivia, and her friends were down to earth, but the popular kids at Park Pendleton seemed more like an exclusive club, and I wanted in.

"Atlas, I want to know what happened last night!" I snapped at him, pulling him out of the trance from the view.

"Easy, easy. You should be thanking me, you were not okay last night. Dizzy was trying to take you up to his room, you almost fell into the pool, so I took you inside to sit down for a little. I went back outside for like a half an hour then the cops showed up at the back gates. It was a herd of people just trampling over each other. More people probably got hurt trying to leave than would have if we just partied all night. Anyways, I carried you out through the front with my friend Sarah; we got you in the car and brought you to my house."

"Did your perv ass change me?" I asked laughing to make it seem like less of a big deal, but I would have been upset if he had said yes.

"No no, you were throwing up a lot, we snuck you into my house but you threw up all over yourself and you were being way too loud so we grabbed some of my clothes and took you out to the garage, Sarah changed you and then I took her home. I don't understand how you're still alive, you were chunking bucket fulls," he said. All I could do was laugh and thank him, but my cheeks went red. I was the girl too drunk to walk. I had to be babysat. I thanked him over and over while we sat there, each time getting a "you're welcome, it's fine though seriously." or some sort of variation. We talked a bit more. He told me how his uncle had left him his mustang in his will before he passed from thyroid cancer. I told him how Tommy Lee gave me his black mustang when he bought himself a new car after the move. I put air quotes around gave because he still took it out to drive whenever he wanted. We sat for a bit longer and blasted music before deciding to leave.

"You ready to go home?" he asked, turning to me.

I told him it was up to him.

He flashed me a great white smirk, his teeth were as icy as his car.

"You said you like *The Great Gatsby* right?"

I nodded.

"Would you be against a Gatsby sesh at my house? We can get Chinese."

His eyes widened and his smile grew from ear to ear.

"Gatsby and Chinese? That sounds like a date hun."

"Hey, you said date, not me," he said.

I thought on it, giving in after only a few seconds. He did save me from drowning in my own vomit and a nice fat underage drinking charge.

"Fine."

We took our time driving home, swapping through songs the whole way. I realized that Tommy Lee hasn't called or texted once to see how I was or what time I was coming home. I opened up to Atlas a lot quicker than I expected.

He just had such a warm and accepting feel to him, like you could tell him the most awful thing you've ever thought, and in turn, he would tell you the same or make something up just as bad just so you didn't feel alone. It wasn't long before we had the windows down, screaming the songs out loud like we were alone in our room. He reached over and silenced the music, leaving only my screeching voice to fill the car.

"How come you haven't asked yet?" He said looking over.

"Asked what?"

"My hair, I know you want to ask."

To be honest it hadn't crossed my mind, obviously, I noticed when I looked at him, but I was so caught up in the hangover and the view and the music that I hadn't really cared either way. But now that he brought it up, I was dying to know.

"It's not really a big deal, I'm not embarrassed," he followed up.

"My friend told me you had a disease."

"Errr. Incorrect. My mother actually has thyroid cancer too, like my uncle. She lost her hair from the treatment."

Well, don't I look like a dick?

"She's pretty insecure about it like most people would be, so I shave my head a couple times a week, just so she doesn't have to do it alone."

Oh. My. God. My heart melted. It melted, and then the molten liquid leftover melted into plasma, evaporating into nothingness.

"YOU ARE AMAZING!" I cried out.

"Stop."

"NO THAT'S SO AMAZING, YOU'RE SUCH A SWEETHEART!"

"Meh, but just a heads up when we get here, just don't stare at her head, she gets upset. Just don't bring it up period, pretend like you don't know what cancer is. As far as you're concerned it's a myth," he said as his serious tone turned to a chuckle.

"Oh my, don't even worry, that's just so awwweee!"

He smiled at me and turned the music back up. I couldn't stop though, that's just the most beautiful thing. I don't even answer my mom's calls but he sacrifices possibly the biggest part of his appearance for his. Textbook mama's boy. It was at that very point in time that my faith in humanity had been restored. But only for a short time.

Making it through the city was rough. The average driver in downtown Park Pendleton was a blood-crazed ass-rider, fed up with their awful nine to five job and living paycheck to paycheck, deciding to take their misery out on other drivers by leaving less than a foot between the poor soul in front of them. This created a chain of one foot spaced drivers moving throughout the city at a snail pace, taking their time to flip off and curse out whoever they felt like. Even though I wasn't driving, my nerves were very high strung, and more than a few times I jerked from my seat or grabbed onto the "oh shit" handle. What scared me the most was that Atlas carried on grandly as if this was one of the safer days in town.

We pulled up to his house, tucked away outside of the north part of the city. The trees surrounding the property looked like a massive wall, cutting them off from the inner city. When we pulled up the driveway you no longer smelled the money and grit of downtown. Instead, it smelled like home. We pulled back into the garage that I woke up in.

"Alright, what's the game plan?" I asked.

"We're gonna go in, you gotta smile all big and pretty and say hi, feel free to make quick small talk. They appreciate that stuff, then its Gatsby time."

"Sounds like a plan."

"Wait," he said grabbing my shoulder. "Whatever you do, don't stare at her head, it's very shiny, and there's a slight chance you'll see your reflection. Just. Eye contact. Pretend she's got the most luscious hair you've ever seen." He was laughing so I knew there was humor in what he said, but I also could tell he was pretty serious about it.

"Don't you think they'll notice I'm, hmm I don't know, wearing your clothes?" I asked him. We look at each other and burst out laughing.

"That may be a minor setback. We could try to sneak you past them, skip the whole introduction thing altogether," he said, looking to see what I thought of the idea.

"No," he followed up before I could answer. "Just follow me."

I trailed him out of the garage and up around the back of his house to a set of two bushes on either side of a small window. He told me to wait there and was off around the corner before I could ask why. I sat balled up between the bushes, staring off into the woods behind his house. A few minutes passed and the window I was sitting against slid up. I was startled but calmed down when I saw Atlas through the window passing me my clean clothes.

"Hurry and change," he whispered. "Don't worry I'll close my eyes."

He disappeared and I pulled down my pants. I tried to pull my leg out but my shoe got stuck in the foot hole, making me fall into the bush.

"The hell you doing?" He whispered.

The sliding back doors to his house opened. A deeper raspy voice spoke to the panting breath and pitter patter of small paws on their back porch. His dad.

"Go on boy, c'mon, go pee," his father called.

The pittering and pattering of the paws drew closer. I turned around, pushing my face into the bush. No no no. A small nose pressed into my back, sniffing me up and down. Please, please don't bark.

"What're ya doin' boy?"

He sniffed me a moment more and lifted his leg. I covered my mouth as he peed all over Atlas' sweatpants. Then he sniffed me again and licked my arm before running back around the corner up onto the porch. The door shutting sprung me into action. I ripped the pants off as fast as I could and tossed them onto the bush across from me. I used the non-pee side of the pants to wipe my ankle off. God forbid his dad walk up on me right now, half naked, rolling in the dirt, holding back tears. I put the rest of my clothes on.

"Atlas?"

"Huh?" he said as he poked his head around the corner.

I tossed the piss pants at him, "courtesy of your pup."

"What the? Gross! C'mon pull me up."

We tossed the other clothes down through the window then snuck around to the front. He brought up his mother's hair one time, reminding me to pretend I've never even heard of cancer, and as far as I knew, she had a full head of hair. I thought it was sweet that he was so protective of his mom. I assured him I'd never even heard of cancer until he brought it up; he laughed then opened the door.

"Mothhaaa, fatthaaa, I've brought a guest!" he called out.

He had a small, but very nicely decorated split level house. The beige walls blended with the smell of cinnamon cookies that filled the house as we walked up into the living room. The inside was gorgeous, you could tell they took care of and appreciated what they had. His mother walked out from the hallway. She was beautiful. The skin of an angel, she looked as though she was the one giving the house the cinnamon cookie smell. She didn't wear makeup or fancy clothes but she had a smile, like Atlas', that told you she was compassionate and a great listener, and that she would do anything she could to help you feel comfortable.

"Oh, honey, so nice to meet you, what's your name dear?" she asked me.

"Blake Hutton," I told her going to shake her hand.

"That is such a pretty name! I don't think I've ever heard that before, but I love that!"

I tried not to blush, but I couldn't help it, I turn red at any compliment.

"Is that a girl?" his father called from back the hall.

His mother answered yes.

"Bullshit." He ran out to the living room to see for himself.

"Well I'll be damned, and a good one at that."

I blushed harder.

"This is Blake Hutton." his mother introduced me.

"Hutton? You grow up here? What's your father's name?" he asked.

"My father's Tommy, he grew up here, but we just moved back."

"Oh, Tommy's your father huh? He was a grade ahead of me. Small world. He was one hell of a fullback. Dude could pick you up and carry you to the locker room. Hell, I think he might've done it one time."

We talked to a bit longer about Richmont Caramel and why we moved back, I explained the divorce but left out the affair and his mother really seemed to feel for me. She just smiled and smiled the whole time, the surprised look never left either of their faces. My eyes roamed their house while we talked. They had family pictures and little signs everywhere, you know the "Live, Laugh, Love" kind of signs. They seemed like they were very close and thankful. I wondered how much of that was from her cancer.

His room was awesome, boyish but awesome. They converted the entire basement into like a mini apartment for him, he had his own shower and a bar with a fridge, microwave, and sink. His bed sat at the far end of the room while the other end was like a living room. A couch sat against one wall with a huge bookshelf and a table with a record player. He had the first six star wars movie posters framed around his room, and while I wasn't much of a space nerd, I could still appreciate it. There was no way to describe his room, it wasn't just modern or just nerdy, it was if his personality just threw up all over the walls and it dried as cool shit. He pulled *The Great Gatsby* DVD out of his library and popped it in the tray. The opening scene and sound of Nick Carraway's voice made Atlas light up.

He respectfully sat on the other side of the couch but we shared a blanket, not once did he try to make any moves which was fine with me. I still didn't even know this guy. But there wasn't a sense of awkwardness at all. He didn't seem pressured to make a move; he was comfortable sitting over there and enjoying the movie. He was completely comfortable as himself which I admired to an envious degree. It didn't take long before our conversation took center stage over the film. We watched it but couldn't go more than five minutes before making jokes and busting out into random side conversation. I can't remember ever talking this much to anyone before. Even my old friends from Richmont Caramel were just people I hung out with to kill time. He was excited and intelligent. I wanted to get lost in our conversations, wrap up in them and never even try to find my way out. The scene of Gatsby reaching across the bay to the green light sparked more conversation.

"So what's yours?" He asked me.

"My..?"

"Green light of course."

"Oh." The question rattled me. What was my purpose? I woke up only looking forward to going back to bed. I had only a faint idea of what I wanted to go to college for, but even that wasn't my ultimate life goal.

"I guess I just keep on keepin on in a way," I answered.

"That doesn't seem like any way to go through the best years of our life."

"Best years huh? Are you insinuating that you're going to peak in high school?"

"Well no, when I say best, I mean easiest. We gotta be big kids in a couple months. What are you thinking about doing after school?"

"Well, I've always wanted to be an English teacher. I just love books, and I think the influence they can have on people is beautiful. There's a book for everything."

"So what's holding you back?" he asked.

"I mean it would be a dream to teach literature and influence young kids, and don't

think of me badly for this, but I just feel like their underpaid."
He smiled.

"What?" I asked.

"Don't you know you're supposed to do what you love and the rest will take care of itself?"

"I know I know," I told him, "And I know that money doesn't buy happiness and yadda yadda I know, I know. I just feel like you gotta be realistic about stuff and I need a job that can one hundred percent support me.

"Fifty or sixty grand a year is nothin' to laugh at though, and why can't that be realistic? You're the only one in your way. Sorry, I'm not tryna go all Tony Robbins on you and give you the "follow your dreams" speech. I just think that's a great job and you'd be great at it."
Oh shit. The red cheeks were back for a guest appearance.
All I could squeeze out from my smile was a small "Thanks." but it carried the weight of a lot more.

"What about you Mr. Life Coach? What is your green light? Your orgastic future that recedes before you?" I asked.
A smile strung across his face like the opening of a curtain, revealing his frosted teeth.

"Good question. I think it's the cancer. I... I just want her to survive this and come out on

top, ten times stronger. No matter the outcome, I want her to live every second acting like she's never even heard of cancer, that nothing can hold her back. I always tell her that time doesn't matter; the moment she wakes up she needs to know that god's blessed her with another day here and it's up to her on what to do with it. We take it day by day."
Damn. He made my eyes water.

"Oh my gosh, what's wrong?" he asked as he sprung to comfort me.

"No nothing that's just beautiful. There's nothing sweeter than a boy that loves his mama." I told him, partly because it was true, the other part was me thinking about my mom.
The movie couldn't last long enough. Eventually, we finished it and went upstairs for dinner. On the way out of his room, my eyes caught on a towering grandfather clock that sat next to his bookshelf. I didn't notice it earlier when we walked it. The clock read six o'clock. I asked if it was the right time and he told me, no, but the time was close to six. When I asked him why he hasn't gotten the clock fixed he told me he doesn't care about the time on the clock, the piece is cool and that's all that matters. I respected that a lot. His parents cooked us a full course meal for dinner. I'm upset it didn't last long though. I went to their bathroom to wash my hands and my face before dinner when my phone started ringing. My

mom. I declined, but I couldn't help but wonder what she would say if I did pick up. The thought nested in me. I wished things were different. I had a weak spot for her, somewhere tucked deep under the layers of resentment for splitting our family up.
No Blake.
You don't have a weak spot. Not for her. Not for cheaters. I threw some water and a fake smile on my face. Before the bathroom door closed behind me, I was crying. Atlas was in the hall waiting for me, he looked at me and took my hand without question, grabbing his keys and guiding me out the front door.

"Hey guys, I forgot but I promised Blake's dad that she would be home earlier, thank you for making us dinner, we appreciate it." He called to them, shutting the front door before they could answer. He opened my car door for me. The small but tremendous gesture still counted for a lot in my book. Looking back, he probably thought I didn't appreciate it because I didn't acknowledge it, but I was just too busy drowning in my tears and family issues. He was right, chivalry wasn't dead. Not yet.

"You want to talk about it?" he asked me.
"Where are we going?"
"You'll see."
We didn't say another word. Which, in a way was kind of nice. Sometimes all you need is

somebody to just be there, physically. It's nice to have that person to rant to, but they never really listen, and if they do they just answer with their own stories of similarities and try to explain how they understand and that they've been in your shoes. But no, you don't understand, you may have had similar things happen to you but you don't get it, our situations are still different. I think he got this because he did the best thing anybody could do. He turned the music up louder and put his hand on my hand. And while, at this point, he was still a stranger to me, there were worse things in the world than a nice guy with a pretty face.

We followed a winding road up to a fortification of trees. The cul de sac. But the earlier view of the mountains was overtaken by the brilliance of downtown. The lights reached out to me, drying my tears and replacing my hurt with excitement. There wasn't any time to be upset about the problems I couldn't fix. I could only control what was in front of me.

"It's really something, ain't it?" he asked.

"It's more than something. I want to be down there, running through the lights."

"I don't know, I feel like some things aren't as pretty from the inside, yeah it looks beautiful, but that's just cause were up here looking down on it. It's peaceful up here, but down there you've got muggings and car accidents. I'd take this any day. You feeling any better?"

"Yeah, a little bit."

"Well, that's not good enough." He said as he got out of the car and ran around to my side, opening up the door with his becoming signature smile.

"What are you doing?"

"What?" He asked laughing, "Ohh, oh god you thought that was the reason we came up here?" He was pointing out to the city. "No no no no no, this is the real attraction," he said, ushering his hand behind me. I got out to look. The trees. They lit up in a coruscating show that melted away every ounce of bad and unfair. Thousands of tiny lights, sputtering in the branches of the trees. It was like looking into the stars. I was in awe, not just from the fireflies, but from Atlas.

He put his hand out, "Well are you gonna sit there or are you gonna come catch some fireflies with me?"

I grabbed his hand and we took off into the trees like too young kids whose worries were reduced to small things like getting home in time for dinner or remembering to do our spelling homework. We snatched and grabbed and collected handfuls, and we still hadn't scratched the surface of the surface of how many fireflies were out with us. They landed on our hands and crawled in our hair. Kissing our skin with clairvoyance. Atlas ran back to the car to grab a water bottle and a pocket knife and poked holes in the cap to catch them with. We collected a small community of them, filled the bottle with grass and a small stick for them to climb on, and then buckled them into the back seat for safe travel. He opened my door for me to get back in.

"Thank you," I told him.

"Oh, it's nothing."

"No, I mean for this, for making me forget about everything, I feel like a little girl again, playing in my backyard. I didn't mean to get all emotional earlier. It's just, you know my parents are split up and I was in the bathroom and my mother called and then your family made dinner and you guys--
He pressed his lips into mine. And I pressed mine back.

"I'm so sorry, you're just so--

"Stop," I told him. "Don't apologize."
then I leaned in to kiss him again. He rubbed his fingers through my hair and I grabbed him, holding him tight. What the hell was I doing? I pulled away but saved myself with a smile.

"Jeez, and she's got a perfect smile."
I smiled harder.

"Just when I thought it couldn't get any better, she smiles."

I ran my tongue across my teeth, feeling the flaws and crookedness. I leaned back in for one more peck before we drove home.

He walked me to my door and I hugged him and thanked him for the entire day and for saving my life. He waited until I got inside and closed the door before leaving. I immediately checked down in the basement for Tommy Lee. He hadn't checked on me at all. I found him, passed out in his recliner, smelling of whiskey. A bottle, with about an eighth left, sat next to him. The smell alone was enough to make me sick again, but seeing it in front of me brought back Vietnam flashbacks from last night. I took the bottle and threw it away upstairs, and then climbed into bed, nesting myself in my covers, where I fell asleep with a smile stretching ear to ear.

CHAPTER SIX

Sunday flew by. I stayed in bed for most of the day binge-watching Netflix, only getting up for bathroom breaks and food. Liv texted me, telling me to check twitter. Kids were tweeting about Dizzy's party. It consumed my entire timeline. Most of them were from other people whose names I hadn't heard of yet.

"Who else couldn't get out of bed after that?" forty-two likes.

"Special guest appearance from the pigs, coulda just asked if you wanted to party too" sixty likes.

"Who else was hyped to see lampshade?" seventy likes, twenty-two replies.

"New girl wasn't holding back last night #queenofthekeg"
I went bug-eyed.
One hundred and twelve likes.
In the comments was a video of me, on my knees, chugging away. I was too excited at the moment

to care about the video getting out or future employers pulling it out asking me to explain. My phone notified me that somebody tweeted at me. I clicked the notifications and it took me to the comments of the video. I read through them.

"New girl looks fire."
"She bad."
"Very bad."
"Who got her number?"
"Ask Dizzy ;)"
"Somebody @ her."
"@blakeyhuttonn"
"Hey Blakeyyy"

What was going on? I'll tell you what was going on. People are talking about me. Apparently, I'm "bad", which was a term I was could've sworn had negative connotations, but I now know is a highly regarded compliment here. Park Pendleton was making me rethink and question everything I've known. They like me here, I think. I'd have to learn to breathe and eat all over again, the way they do it here. I texted Liv, "they're talkin about me!" to which she replied, "go you mate!"
I refreshed the feed every minute for the next hour, reading every new comment and answering back to guys. Soon other tweets about "the new girl" filled Twitter. I was blowing up. My message box had new names in it every couple of minutes. I sat there an hour longer rolling down through everything, dizzy even tweeted

something about me. Atlas texted me. Wait. He texted me. His contact was in my phone?

"Mornin, mind if I drop a gift off?" he asked.

He must have put it in my phone Friday night. I was probably drunk enough to unlock my phone and hand it over to a complete stranger. I didn't question it. I typed a text back to him, "If you can remember where I live ;)" but stopped myself before I sent it. Kennedy has guys flocking to her. She walked up to whoever she wanted to at the party and kissed them. What would she do? I messaged her on twitter.

Kennedy?
Yes, dear?
Cute guy, how do I deal with him?
Hard to get.

That was all I needed to hear. I felt bad for it, but I didn't text him back the entire day. He was so so nice to me yesterday, and when we kissed I felt something. A small something, but a something nonetheless. It doesn't matter; Kennedy knows what she was talking about. I felt a little bad about myself, I kissed him back, I gave him hope. Then I stomped all over it when he watched my text bubble pop up and disappear right after. I read some more tweets for another twenty minutes, I had gained seventy some followers since I had woken up, after I put Netflix on and relaxed all night, falling asleep early.

I got up early Monday morning with a new found excitement for school. All of the anxiety I had surrounding it seemed to have disappeared. I put on my favorite shirt, a giant yellow smiley face, simple but a classic. Exactly how I was feeling. I threw on a pair of acid washed jeans and rolled the bottoms up. I checked my phone before heading downstairs to say goodbye to Tommy Lee. The video kept blowing up, the last notification came in at four something in the morning. Who was up at four? Especially on a school night. The video. Three hundred and twenty-two likes. Atlas didn't text me anymore which was kind of upsetting but I got over it after remember that I did leave him on read after all. Tommy Lee was downstairs in his boxers making waffles with a beer in hand. His drinking had picked up since the divorce, but it didn't bother me. I could only imagine what he was going through. He offered me some waffles, as I was walking out the door, knowing it's not like I was going to turn around and come back in to sit down and eat. It had been a couple days since I'd been behind the wheel of my beauty. The leather steering wheel, the leather seats. Not as comfy as Atlas', but still comfy enough to make me consider skipping the first two periods and sleep on them in the student lot. I couldn't skip, that's two wasted periods where I could see Atlas in the halls. On the drive to school, the anxiety returned.

Not for school itself, but just for what I would say to Atlas when I saw him. Do I ignore the fact that we sucked eat others faces off two nights before? Or do I act as I had never even seen his message yesterday, even though it clearly says that I read it? I tried to create mental notes of small talk. What his favorite classes were? His favorite teachers? If he was going to the party this week? It all felt too forced. I was getting too far ahead of myself. How would I even say hi? Hey. Hi. Yo. Whatsup? Hello. I felt like he was more of a hello guy.

Despite waking up and getting out the door early, the lot was near full when I got there, I drove past lines and lines of cars before finding a spot. I parked and found my place in the bottleneck of students funneling in through the doors. I climbed the stairs and waddled past everyone down the halls to my locker, getting stares from groups of people the entire time. I grabbed my books and shut my locker door to find Olivia's face smiling behind it.

"Ello there, care for a nana?" She asked, putting a banana on top of my books. "It's the most important meal of the day ya know?"

"Thanks, I guess."

We walked to first period together while I filled her in on the Atlas situations.

"YOU WHAT? WHY WOULDNT YOU TEXT HIM BACK?" She screamed.

"Thanks, Liv, maybe next time remember his name when you scream it for everyone to hear."
We laughed.
I told her it was Kennedy's advice and she rolled her eyes. We walked to class and plotted out plans for the week, settling on a theft-free trip to the mall Thursday and after joyriding around town to find something to do. She asked me about seeing the new Blood Horizon movie that came out that night. Blood Horizon was the final installment of blood-sucking seductive vampires against zombies love trilogy that was perfectly marketed to girls like me and Olivia. It held pretty much zero actual artist value as far as cinematography goes, but I can admit I had seen the first two and I was dying to find out how it would end. The final movie had been in production for three years and left every girl I knew waiting with wide eyes and drooly mouths to see it. Tickets were already being reserved and were close to sold out so she said she would text me later that night to buy them. We got to Mr. Ravensworth's class where he asked me if I had acquired any sudden chemistry or science-related interests yet, to which I answered "Not yet, but you'll be the first to know when I do." the class flew by, but that was mostly due to my daydreams and rehearsal of conversation starters for Atlas.

Mikey P caught up with me in the halls on our way to Dr. Leeland's class.

"Queen of the keg chug huh?"

"I guess that's me." I told him.

"It's pretty crazy how big that tweet got, I heard a couple people talking about you today."

"Really?" I asked, "like what?"

"I forgot I just heard your name, anyways though that's a big honor, be prepared to defend your title this Friday."

"This Friday?"

"Yeah this Friday," he told me, "it's at my buddy Kevin's house, I'll introduce you."

I didn't know if I could handle another party in this city, but I told him I would be there anyway. I left him to seek out Kennedy, who was touching up her makeup in her locker mirror. She saw me walking towards her and turned to me.

"Hey there sweetie! Who is the cute boy by the way?"

I told her it was Atlas Lightner, she looked disgusted.

"The... the bald kid? I don't think I've ever talked to him, I thought he was some weirdo. You really like him, Blakey?"

"I don't know. He's a total weirdo I guess I just hung out with him so he could buy me lunch." I told her, cringing at my own lies.

"I like it girl, dig for that gold. Here's a tip for ya. That outfit. Yuck. we can go shopping this week to get you something new, just promise me you're going to go home and burn that shirt." I told her okay. And that I woke up late and threw it on to get to school on time. I was beyond embarrassed. I thought about leaving school or just going home to change, I couldn't walk around the rest of the day like that. If she thought that, then what was everyone else thinking of me. I held my tears back, I couldn't be upset, she was just trying to help, I had to take her advice. She knew best.

English with Mr. Brubaker seemed like it was going to be the only class I would enjoy. He had a real passion for literature, it was more than just words on a page to him, it was stories, people's history, recollection of actual emotions that were actually felt by actual people. He wanted us to look at it the same way. His eyes lit up when I told him I enjoyed to write. Later towards the end of class, he ended his lesson abruptly to call me out in the hall where I thought over everything I could have possibly done to get reprimanded on my second day.

"I would love you to send me a piece. It doesn't have to be something too personal, heck, it can be some tapped together book you made in kindergarten." he told me.

"I uh, I don't know." I said rubbing my arm looking away.

"You have my word it will never be under the eyes of anybody but me. I just enjoy reading my students pieces. Just think about it, I'll write down my email for you when we go back in. If anyone asks why I called you out, you can just tell them I was asking how you think you'll do in this class. Which, by the way, I think you'll do great."

He didn't say anything else to me; we went back into class where everyone was up out of their seats in their own groups, screaming over each other to talk. Sure enough, he wrote me his email and slipped it on my books as I was leaving class. I ran to lunch to avoid the crowd. The lunch rush wasn't any less chaotic despite being five minutes early. I grabbed a chicken salad and checked out, stepping off to the side after to wait and see where Atlas checked out. People shoved passed and told me to move. There were way too many people in the way to watch all six of the registers.

"Waiting for someone?"

I jumped around; tilting my tray but a hand with a leather band watch grabbed the side of my tray, steadying it.

"Look, I told you I'd forgive you for my favorite shirt, but the second shirt's gonna cost you."

Atlas.

He had a bright smile on.

"Oh, hey." I said, clearing my voice. I planned out the perfect hello and practiced all day and royally messed it up.

"So, you gonna eat your salad or keep people watching?" he asked, "Because although I probably wouldn't list people watching under my likes and interests, it is a favorite pastime of mine."

"It's alright, let's go sit down." I told him. We walked over to his table, passing Liv's table on the way where she flashed me a wink and a big thumbs up. I sat at his table with him, Sarah, and his other friends who he introduced. I forgot their names instantly, but this time because I wasn't even listening, I just got caught up in his smile. My nerves vanished after chiming in a couple times to their conversation. They seemed like they were trying to include me in and asked for my opinion on everything they brought up. Leaving lunch he stopped me.
"I love that shirt oh my god!"
"Really?" I asked.
"Yeah, it's cute on you. All bright and smiley, just like its wearer."
Shit. I was blushing again.
"and one more thing. Thursday, what's your schedule look like? If it's open, I wanna book you."
"Yes! Totally! Just tell me when!"

"You sure? Totally optional. But if you say no I'm still picking you up anyway. So. Totally optional.

"No kidnapping needed." I told him.

We broke off back to our classes, both of us with beating hearts and smiles bright enough to power a neon sign that read "love is in the air".

Later that night I texted Atlas, just to ask what plans he had in store. I got no answer about that from him, but it did spring on a three-hour conversation. Each text going in and out every thirty seconds. We must have sent hundreds. I couldn't even tell you what we were talking about. It was just talk. Not forced, it just flowed out. He texted as intelligently as he spoke, and I could read every message in his articulated voice. Liv interrupted with a call.

"Aye mate, so tickets, you wanna log on to buy them?" she asked me.

"Uh oh. Small but actually kind of big problem. I promised Atlas I would do something Thursday night. I'm sorry, don't wait up for me, just go with everyone else. I'm so so sor—"

"Don't even worry about it."

"Seriously?"

"Yeah it's just a movie. You go girl! Have fun, I want to hear every detail after."

"Of course," I told her. "Thanks for understanding."

We hung up and I submerged myself back into my text bubbles and spelling errors from typing too fast. We talked for another hour, and then he asked to facetime before we went to bed. I thought back to what Kennedy had said. Hard to get. At the pace I was going, I was opening my gates, unlocking my doors, and handing over the keys for him to steal my heart. I respectfully declined and told him I was tired and was just going to get to bed now. He was alright with that.

CHAPTER SEVEN

The next two days couldn't pass fast enough. I went to the mall with Olivia and Cassandra Tuesday night to make up for skipping the movie on Thursday. I decided to make an honest effort to start referring to Cassandra by her real name and not some variation of a bull. We had a lot of fun, theft free fun. At least I think so, maybe that serves as a true testament to how good of a thief the bull, or recently renamed "Cassandra," really is.

My Wednesday was simply twenty-four hours of nail biting anxiety of my date to come. It's no exaggeration when I say for three plus hours I rocked myself to sleep on my floor, pillow under my head. My thoughts began to spiral around me, one thought led to another. I alluded it to a set of dominoes lined up shakily stringing down into a dark hallway. The anxiety sparked, and I say that as if there was one singular moment that a switch was just flipped and next thing I knew, I lost my mind, but sadly it's never that easy for me. Instead, it usually creeps up on me. I start to feel as though I'm just losing a connection to the objects and world around me and then my radical breathing usually alerts me to it. From there my thoughts are wherever they chose to go; my ship sets sail into a dangerous sea of unrealistic worries and thoughts not worth thinking but are usually thought anyways.

So there I lay rocking myself. I felt as though I had lost control, and when you find yourself in situations like this, there's no magic syringe with an antidote you can stick into your thigh for instant relief. There's nobody to go to, at least not for me. If I did go to somebody, I'm not sure this would be something I could describe, or that there is anything to even be done. I don't remember the first time that I ever even had an anxiety attack. They just became a part of life that I accepted and tried to welcome in in an effort to speed up the process. I sat up and wiggled my toes for a good minute until I was positive that I had total control over them. Next, I shook my feet back and forth, extending and retracting my legs. After I did the same with my fingers, hands, and arms. After becoming so devoted to the moving of limbs and phalanges, I had realized I was back in control. My breathing had calmed and I was absolutely fine, which drove me even crazier. What if I was actually fine the entire time? I had a tendency of thinking myself into slumps. I take a situation that has no business being dissected, and I pick at every word said in the conversation and the body language and possible outcomes and soon I have myself in a prison of thoughts. After wiggling my chains off I climbed in bed, nervous but excited for Thursday.

I woke the next morning and sped through my morning routine: shower, do my hair, pick out my clothes. I put a lot of effort into this. Kennedy's clothes were scandalous, revealing, screaming wild card. I didn't have anything like that in my closet. I wore what I thought she would like the best. A maroon long sleeved tight shirt with a slightly cropped stomach and black jeans, accompanied by a push up bra. I looked in the mirror, it made, well it made me pop for sure. Too much pop, though. I didn't want to be falling out of my shirt the whole day, so I switched bras. I looked damn good, but I didn't look much like myself. But I looked good, so I forced myself away from the mirror. It didn't matter, there was no possible way Atlas, or any guy in the school, would be able to take his eyes off of me. I brushed my teeth and thought about trying makeup, but it just wasn't me. I had a good bit of makeup I'd purchased with gift cards I got from relatives from Christmas. The epitome of gifts from relatives who barely know you. I could see my aunt and uncle talking about it. "Oh she's a girl, just get her an Ulta gift card." School was long and painful; I counted down every minute until the final bell, where after, I got my ass smacked by some dick in the hall on the way out of school. I sped home and waited for a text or a call or telepathic message from Atlas. Anything really. I applied a healthy serving of deodorant and re-brushed my teeth and sat on my bed waiting. Six o'clock he texted me.

Landing incoming. ETA 5 minutes. Standby.

Roger that. I replied.

One more thing soldier.

Yes?

Listen to my instructions very closely. Bring a big empty purse and ice packs. No questions asked.

What?

Hello? I just said no questions asked. ETA 2 minutes.

I scrambled down the stairs to find a purse. It's not like I could just steal my mom's, and I usually never used one. I ran back up the steps and into my closet, digging past a pile of sneakers and clothes I tore down while deciding on an outfit this morning. I pulled out what might be the ugliest of all handbags. A "Francesco Lane" purse, not even sure what that is, that was a brick red with neon green X's stitched all over it.

Luckily, this was a discrimination-free household when it came to handbags, so this would do the trick.

Your transport has arrived cadet!
I grabbed two ice packs out of the freezer and booked it out the front door. He was waiting out front of the car for me, holding open my door. Atlas had on a tan jacket over top of a gray tight t-shirt. With skinny ripped jeans on, he was one hundred and seventy pounds of god damn. I got in and the door closed, I noticed his hand next to me as he shut it. His leather watch was broken. We whisked away leaving behind a cloud of smoke and screaming to the Bowling for Soup song that he was playing. We decided that the song shouldn't be interrupted, so we took turns singing while the other got in a word.

"SPRINGSTEEN, MADONNA, WAY BEFORE NIRVANA! THERE WAS U2 AND BLONDIE!" he shouted while I asked where we were going.

I finished the chorus. "AND MUSIC STILL ON MTV! HER TWO KIDS IN HIGH SCHOOL, THEY TELL HER THAT SHE'S UNCOOL!" While he insisted I would have to wait and see.

We joined in together to finish, "CAUSE SHE'S STILL PREOCCUPIED WITH 19-19-1985!"

We continued to flip through songs until we pulled into the Walmart in downtown. He slipped into the spot and turned off the car and looked at me smiling.

"I guessed you were a romantic, but I never thought you would have something like this up your sleeve," I told him. "Nobody has ever taken me on a date to Walmart." Nobody has ever taken me on a date at all as a matter of fact, but he didn't need to know that.

"Oh shush," he said, getting out and sliding across the hood of the pearly mustang over to my side where he opened my door for me. "This is the preparation phase."

I followed him into Walmart and down to the freezer aisle where we sat before a wall of ice cream of every flavor, color, and candy.

He looked at me, smiling bigger every time I looked back at him. "Get whatever you want, no less than two."

I scoured the aisle for what must have been fifteen minutes. Picking up ice cream, changing my mind, putting them back down, picking them back up. I chose a weird rainbow colored ice cream with chunks of snickers and skittles and a classic tub of mint chocolate chip in case the first tub sucked. While checking out, I had noticed Atlas got stares from just about everyone we passed, and he seemed aware but unaffected which only added to the person he was. We checked out and headed back to the car.

"Oh, we're early," he said, "still got a half hour to burn."

I went to ask what he wanted to do but before I got the words out of my mouth he was inside the car putting music on and cranking the stereo up as loud as it would go. He left his door open and ran around to the other side to open my door. The rap music blasted throughout the parking lot. The birds flying high overhead chirped along while people loading groceries in their cars around us stopped to stare.

"What are you doing?" I asked him.

"I could ask you the same thing, why aren't you over here dancing?" He asked spinning around and shimmying over to me. I thought for a second about how stupid we looked, and thought about how much he didn't care, that was just one more reason for me to join him. We danced and jumped and spun and everything in between while the music blasted and cars and people continued on around us, leaving us be in our own bubble of whatever this was. He switched the music to some upbeat Mexican salsa dance song and although neither of us knew how to salsa, we sure as hell acted like we did. Thirty minutes passed and we were sweaty, so we hopped in the car and sped off, returning the parking lot to its vast obscurity of loading groceries and returning carts and other adulty chores.

"So we have the ice cream but do we have an actual destination?" I asked Atlas.

"Check the glove box."

I opened the compartment to reveal an envelope.

"Jesus, the suspense, oh it's killing me," I said laughing, he joined in.

"Seriously, open it."

I did.

Two tickets for Blood Horizon.

"WHAT? YOU DID NOT!"

"Oh but on the contrary. I did."

I leaped across the car to hug him, he swerved but steadied.

"Easy, if you don't mind I would like to actually make it to the movies?" He told me.

"Oops. Sorry."

"Don't apologize, just turn the music up!"

And I did and we sung and screamed the whole way to the theatre.

The theatre's lot was loaded, cars in every spot spilling out with girls jumping around and screeching, reciting all of their favorite lines from the first two movies. We parked in the lot of a burger restaurant a block down the street. Walking through the rows Atlas reached down for my hand. I met him halfway.

"So I have to get something off my chest. It's been bugging me for a couple days now," he said, his blue eyes piercing mine. Oh god, what now?

I gave him the look to continue.

"Well. I don't really know how to say this. It's kind of embarrassing, but I feel like it's just something you're gonna have to know about me, and the sooner we get it out of the way the better."

"No no, don't be embarrassed," I told him, "just spill it, you can trust me."

"No like it's really, really embarrassing."

"Atlas…"

"I've never seen any of the Blood Horizon movies."

"WHAT?"

"I'm sorry!"

"I don't know what's worse, that or what I thought you were gonna say."

"Well, what did you think I was gonna say?" he asked me.

"I don't even know. I was ready for anything, but honestly, anything would've been better than that."

"I'm sorry, they say honesty is the best policy, but now I know that's a complete lie."

I shoved him laughing.

"I was gonna try to play it off but all I could think of was you asking me who my favorite character was or to recite my favorite line so I figured I should just give myself up."

"So how did you know I'd wanna see it?"

"What girl doesn't?"

"Fair enough. Consider yourself lucky, I'll let it slide, but if you woulda said that inside, you'd be getting curb stomped by a mob a blood-crazed girls."

He laughed. "Don't act like you wouldn't be right there with them getting your kicks in." The people walking parallel with us to the theatre on the other side of the cars spoke so loud we were pretty much in their conversation. A group of British girls. No. Their accents too eccentric to be real. As we walked I caught a glimpse of Olivia in between the cars with the Bull. No, wait. I mean Cassandra. She was with Cassandra and two other girls. I pulled Atlas back behind the closest car.

"What the he-
I put my hand over his mouth. He licked my hand.

"Eww why would you do that?"

"I'm sorry, it's a built-in defense mechanism. What's wrong though?"

"I told Liv I would see this with them tonight."

"Ohhh. Well, I guess this will be interesting for me after all."

"Should we leave?" I asked.

"Hell to the no we're gonna march on in there and watch zombies and werewolves-

"It's vampires. Zombies and vampires."

"That's what I said. Now let's go."

The inside of the theatre was as bustling as downtown at night, people running, screaming, dramatic renditions of the ending of the second movie played out in every corner. One out of every four people was dressed in full cosplay costume. There they were. Liv and Cassandra dressed in their Elizabeth Vanderblood costumes in line.

I turned to ask him what we should do but he wasn't beside me anymore. He was across the room at a booth that was selling zombie masks. I watched as he knocked over a stack of the masks, apologizing to the worker, then slipped two inside his jacket and swerved in and out of the crowd back over to me.

"There you go m'lady."

Where did this kid come from?

We slipped the masks on and got into line about ten people behind them. I was safe but Atlas was one of maybe twenty guys in the room, and the only bald eighteen-year-old at that.

We made it in undetected and took our seats towards the top row, far above them, so we took our masks off. We got the ice cream tubs out of the purse.

"We supposed to eat with our hands?" I asked.

Atlas whipped out two spoons from his pocket.

"You think I'd plan this and not come prepared?"

"Were those in your pocket?"

"Oh please," he said, "everyone knows germs are a myth."

We were half a container deep when the previews ended and the movie started, revealing Elizabeth Vanderblood slaying undead beasts left and right, fighting her way back through her captured castle to the throne room where her love, Zylander, the ghoul prince of Transylvania was captured by more brain munchers. She made a gory mess of the monsters, slashing and stabbing, Ending in a magical reunion and kiss scene with Zylander that send the entire theatre into a roaring applause. I jumped up with everyone else in the room squealing and turning to hug other girls around me. It didn't matter who was who, we were all Vanderblood sisters. I turned back around and knocked Atlas' ice cream tub back onto him, painting him with mint chocolate chip. He just stared at me. I think he said something but the screaming, clapping, and crying around me drowned him out.

"I AM SOO SORRY!"

"THERE SEEMS TO BE A RECURRING THEME HERE! IT'S A GOOD

THING YOU'RE PRETTY BECAUSE YOU'RE ONE HELL OF A CLUTZ."

Everyone settled back in their seats while I sat mortalized in disbelief at the universes attraction between me and spilling food on cute boys.

"Seriously," I whispered, "I'm so sorry, I'm gonna go get napkins."

"Wait up," he said, scooping his finger into the ice cream and eating it.

"Mhm. Personally, I think it tastes the same, here, try it."

I leaned in to lick it off his finger and he smeared it across my face.

"Big mistake," I told him.

We sat scooping and smothering the ice cream on each other, making a mess of our clothes and the seats.

I left the bag under the seat with the ice cream, it was ruined now, and then I grabbed his hand. I took him out of the theatre, trying to sneak past where Liv and her friends were sitting. We went to the bathroom to wash off. He finished early and waited outside of the girls' room for me. I came out clean and looked up and down the halls. Nobody. I grabbed him, pulling him into the girl's room with me and a whirlwind of kissing and laughing. He lifted me up onto the sink and kissed me. He was so gentle with me, graceful and respectful, but euphoric, this didn't feel like the kiss we shared nights before. His lips seemed softer and pressed harder. It wasn't sexually charged. It was just two kids having fun. Innocent. I didn't want it to be anything more at the moment and he accepted without question. We left the restroom smiling and giggling, hand in hand. We were almost out the front doors when the man from the mask booth stopped us.

"Hey, can I speak with you for a minute sir?"

Atlas told me to go on outside like there was some fight in a nightclub brooding and he didn't want me involved. He came out a minute later all smiley as usual.

"Well?" I asked.

"Let's just say you'd be surprised at the stuff you can get away with when people think you have cancer. I told you, the shiny head has its perks."

CHAPTER EIGHT

The next month could only be described as the best twenty some odd days of my life. Atlas and I had blossomed into something special. I think it was love; I'm slow to throw around the L-word. If used in abundance, it can quickly lose its significance and just be another phrase for "yeah you're pretty cool I suppose." And although I don't think I qualify to have a legitimate opinion on what is love and is not, in fact, he was my only boyfriend so I have no comparison or prerequisite to go off of, but it was the kind of special and love that you could feel coursing through you at any moment. The nervous sweats around him had subsided. Our conversations became deep and brain picky, it was more me picking his brain and learning from him than anything. In fact, there were numerous times when I wondered and even asked him what it was about me that was so special. He was a boy

from another earth, a higher degree of
intelligence and satirical humor that sometimes
left my jaw open, trying to register what it was he
was saying to me until about two minutes later
when I hit the "ohhhh now I got it moment," but
yet he put up with me. At least that's how I saw
it, but he insisted he saw things in me, and he also
insisted his goal was to help me see those things
too. Back to the love. I know I love him because I
find myself thinking about him at moments I
shouldn't. For instance, the party last Friday
when I was drunk and wandering around Clarissa
Sanchez's house in the South Hills, I stumbled in
on a kid in the bathroom puking out every ounce
of food and stomach acid he had. I helped him for
a little bit and wandered off to find him water but
got lost along the way in my thoughts of what
Atlas was doing at that very moment. So I
decided to call him, and got locked into a long-
lasting conversation about God knows what,
leaving the poor toilet boy to fend off his alcohol
poisoning alone. Atlas didn't like parties much,
which is funny because he saved me from one.
He doesn't drink or smoke anything. He knows
I've smoked weed a few times with Kennedy and
once with Olivia, and he was never mad but just
always insisted I text him when I'm home safe or
go to bed wherever it is I'm staying and that I can

call him at any hour and he'll be on his way to get me if I need something. That was just who he was and what made me fall for him so hard. He was the gentlest person I'd ever known, and it was always about me when I was with him. Ignore the corny sickening cliché but he really made me feel like a princess. Every act and word he said was laced with a buried tenderness that said: "I understand you, and if I don't understand you I would like you to help me understand." It didn't take long before I spilled to him the story of my parents' divorce and Tommy Lee's drinking problem which was worsening by the second. He listened and never once said, "I get what you're going through, this happened to me once." No, he knew that you never truly know how somebody feels. It was just him listening and holding me and helping me through it, he never made it about him. Our first time having sex, he asked six times if I was okay and comfortable and if there was anything he could do. And yes I counted how many times because that stuff matters to me.

    I think it's unlikely that a girl ever finds her own Atlas Lightner, he was like a handcrafted angel God sent me to get through these shitty months. It didn't take long before we had the cute lifetime movie love. The kind you think you'll never get because you don't deserve. Well, your girl got it. And damn it was better than I'd ever dreamed off. We had a catalog of our own inside jokes and our own language only we could understand; we had certain looks that said "yes" or "no" or "meet in the bathroom for a make out sesh." I couldn't tell if I was still in the honeymoon stage or not because we never seemed to fight, and that just made me question all the more if he was actually real or not. His bald head had practically disappeared to me. Not that it was something I cared about anyways but now it was just one more piece of him that I loved.

I had hung out with Olivia and Cassandra, and they were always good for old fashioned fun and movie night sleepovers. They were the childhood friends I had always wanted but took eighteen years to get. Olivia had turned into the best friend you meet at summer camp and stay friends ever since, finishing each other's sentences and knowing weird facts about each other like on what exact day and time did you get your period, hers was when she was twelve, it was September sixth at 4:35 pm. Mine was on Christmas Eve when I was fourteen. I was at my parents' friend's house for a Christmas party between nine and ten o'clock and my mom had to save me in the bathroom because I was screaming and crying. I thought I was dying. I can't help it I had always known periods are a thing, but that first time you see blood you can't help but assume it's your time for the lord to claim you. Liv and I crammed all of that into just a month. I always had this weird feeling about her, however, like yes I knew we were best friends and best friends cared about each other, but it was almost like she was obsessed with me but in a non-obsessive way. Excuse how much sense that doesn't make. It's just that she would text me some nights to say goodnight, and when we were with a group of friends and someone would crack a joke, I'd always catch her looking to me to see if we both were laughing, little stuff. But it didn't make me like her any less. I had finally broken into Kennedy's little circle, I'd been invited to her smaller parties that were just a couple of the cheerleaders and football players. Plenty of alcohol. It was somewhat disgusting how the whole group just seemed to take turns sleeping with each other, when that would take place I would bury myself in a corner with my drink and sit on my phone but that never seemed to stop Dizzy from trying to make a move on me. I still couldn't figure him out.

I had gone over to Kennedy's house one night for just a sleepover with her and one other girl, who was a cheerleader named Alexis, the classic blonde beauty who lived in the hills with Kennedy, 4.0 GPA. Her parents insisted on her going to school at Notre Dame because "every member of their family for the last forty years had gone there," but she seemed like that was just all the more reason for her not to want to go. Kennedy's family was nice. Her father was a businessman, out of town most of the week, while her mother was beautiful and skinny, and the more I was over there the more I noticed the way she looked at her tennis coach. Kennedy was mostly raised by her three maids, two older women who didn't seem like taking care of Kennedy was anything more than a paycheck, and one gay servant who she referred to as Uncle Michael. He took her on tea dates when she was little and sparked her love for high fashion. They had a good relationship, and she spoke more words to him in the night of that sleepover than I'd ever heard her say to both of her parents combined. That night I was lying on her bed while she begged to do my makeup.

"Please please please, Blake. Why wouldn't you want to look like us?"

"I'm just not in the mood, my head hurts," I told her. The truth was, I was just in a deep conversation with Atlas about the effects of global warming and how we were both going to drive Tesla's and have a completely solar-powered house. I was really banking on him being the breadwinner in the family.

"You've already taken over my wardrobe Kennedy, and now you're going to invade my face."

"Don't be so dramatic. You're one of twelve girls in our grade who don't wear makeup, and the other eleven are in the band."

"My head just hurts; just give me a couple minutes."

Kennedy gazed over to Alexis and she smiled back.

"Here Blake, I'll go grab you some Tylenol."

She disappeared into her bathroom and returned with an unlabeled bottle. She handed me a small white pill that looked like no Tylenol I'd ever seen. But I figured rich people had access to all of the best medicine.

"This stuff will cure any headache in a half hour, I swear by it."

I opened my mouth and down the hatch it went. The girls smirked at each other.

"I think I have a headache, too," Alexis said.

"Well shit, I'm not being left out." Kennedy said. Then they both took one.

"Why are you guys being so weird?" I asked.

"What do you mean?" Kennedy answered.
"Never mind."

Sure enough, my "headache" was gone a half hour later. Because I couldn't feel my face at all. When I talked, it felt like I heard my own voice in my head which made me stumble over my words.

"What the hell was that?" I asked.
They both giggled.

"How um... what's your thoughts on OxyContin?" Kennedy asked, pulling a pillow over her face.

"WHAT?" I said trying to lunge up from her floor but I couldn't muster up the energy to even sit up.

"Relax it's not bad for you. Like I heard Kanye West takes these throughout the day to make music," she told me.

I didn't even want to argue with her, I just wanted to purge this whole feeling from my body and feel my face again. Kennedy was on the phone with somebody, and when I asked who she just told me her friends. Twenty minutes later Dizzy and Mikey P burst into the room, rum bottle in hand, with another short buff kid named Brock behind them. Dizzy was stoned out of his mind. He swore it made him a better athlete and driver. Which was something you couldn't really argue with; he had scholarships from basically every D1 school you could think of. He had broken the school record set by Tommy Lee's beer buddy Kenny for most touchdowns. I was feeling my face again, but I was still drowsy and chilled out.

They spread out all over the room. Kennedy was in her bed making out with Mikey, they had recently formed a relationship, although I'd seen Kennedy with a catalog of other guys the first two weeks since they become official. Brock and Alexis weren't together or anything, but she was just the go-to girl for the football team. That left Dizzy and me. He snuck up behind me while I was sitting on the beanbag I'd dragged to the middle of the room and snatched my phone from my hand.

"Who you texting, boo?" he asked, as he scrolled through Atlas' and my messages.

"Nobody, give it back." I lunged for my phone.

"You're gonna have to come get it," he said running into Kennedy's bathroom.

"What are we five?" But he had shut the door, and I knew he wasn't giving it back. The last thing I wanted was him texting Atlas or reading our conversations about global warming. So I went in after him. Which led to two of the worst mistakes I'd ever made.
I entered the bathroom and he jumped out of the shower, wrapping me up in the curtain.

"GET OFF ME!" I screamed.

"Okay damn chill chill, why you wildin like that I'm just messing with you?" he said.

"You need to chill, let's take an Oxy together."

"No, I'm alright." And really I was, I think a sixteenth of one would've done the trick.

"Too late. Don't leave me hanging I'm just tryna have fun with you. I think you're actually pretty cool for real," he said getting her pill bottle of from under the sink. He put one up to my mouth, and I saw Atlas saying no and then I saw Dizzy saying yes.

"Don't you wanna have fun?" he asked me.
I swallowed the pill, which was mistake number one.
He never took one with me.
We went back to the bean bag and talked for a while. We talked about school; I told him I wanted to be a writer, and he said I'd be a good one. He told me he was going to the league no doubt, just like his father. Which was crazy to me, I'm sitting next to a future NFL player. I took oxy with a future NFL player. Well, I guess a future NFL player watched me take oxy. Throughout our conversation, he kept throwing in small compliments like how pretty my blonde hair was and how naturally beautiful I was without makeup. He started to run his fingers through my hair. He stopped talking like a hood rat and started being really nice to me.

"Great idea!" he told me.
"I love a great idea."

"Brock and Alexis finished off the rum, but Kennedy told me where she stashes some of her alcohol," he said.

"Oooh where?"

"Just follow me." He took my hands and stumbled me through the hallway down to the guest room. I followed him in and he shut the door behind me. I knew there was no alcohol in there.

Which was mistake number two.

He threw me on the bed and climbed on top off me, kissing me up and down my neck. I didn't even tell him to stop. I didn't even think about telling him to stop. I didn't think about Atlas or what he would think or what he was doing at the moment. Maybe if I did I would've fallen into one of my trances and got up and left the room to call him and talk. But I didn't. I let him kiss me. And after a few seconds, I kissed him back. I hated myself for thinking that I liked it. Because in the moment, he felt good and he made me feel good, and I hate myself for it. He got up and shut off the lights.

The next morning I lay on Atlas' bedroom floor fumbling through the books on his case. I picked away at the skin around my thumbnail until it was raw and pink and bloody. There was only one question on my mind, do I tell? And if I do, how? He was sitting on his bed, finishing the last episode of Star Wars the Clone Wars season five. I would look over and catch him tapping on the glass of his broken watch. The balance of right and wrong teetering back and forth in my head. It was selfish not to tell him. I knew that. The way I looked at it, it meant nothing, and if it did mean even a little bit I would force myself to make it mean nothing. I wanted to tell him, but I thought it would just cause more bad than good. It was never going to happen again and that's all that mattered. His bookshelf was lined up in alphabetical order by title, ignoring the beginning "the" in the name of most of the books. Two rows down I found the Holy Bible. I pulled it out and opened it up to find markings and circlings all thought it. Almost the entire thing had been drawn in.

"Do we have a little Bible thumper here?" I asked him.

"Funny funny."

"No seriously, have you like read this whole thing?"

"Yeah," he said.

"That's commitment. What's your favorite book in it?" I asked.

"None of them. Don't take that in a dark way, I just don't know where I stand on it."

"Why is that?"

This was a question he took seriously; he stopped tapping on his watch and looked up at me.

"I don't know, I guess you could say me and faith had a falling out after... after my mom got diagnosed."

"Oh, I'm sorry I didn't mean to bring it up."

"No it's okay, you wanted to know."

"You don't believe everything happens for a reason? I know it's hard to make sense of it, especially with her circumstances, but you don't think there's anybody above watching over you?"

"You know, I believe in creationism. I think the universe is too vast and beautiful, it has to be handcrafted. This place didn't happen by accident, that I'm sure of. But the Bible itself and the story it tells I just find to be far-fetched. Not that the fact that we're living on a floating rock hurtling through space at a thousand miles an hour isn't far-fetched. I don't know, I don't think God created one man to die for us and set us free. How can he be a fair and morally right god if he lets my mother die? What about Ted Bundy? Or the thirty some girls he killed? Does that mean the girls were put on this earth to live their entire life until Ted brutally murdered them? That's where they fit into all of this? And Ted was put here to cause years of grief and pain to the families of those girls? Or what about the kids in South Africa who are enslaved and forced to mine blood diamonds? Were they put here for that sole reason? To live in captivity? It doesn't sound like much of an almighty god to me."

"Yeah, I guess you're right," I told him. He was rubbing his watch while he spoke.

"I think it's naive that there are many religions and each one thinks theirs is right. You know there are prehistoric caves with human paintings of dinosaurs? Not just fossils but actual paintings of dinosaurs with skin and muscle on them? How were dinosaurs just left out of the Bible if Adam and Eve were supposed to be the first humans, but there's proof we've been here for millions of years. I'm not saying like I don't believe in God. I just don't think that there's a Christian God who's "fair" and a "great savior".

"So what god do you believe in?" I asked him. I loved these moments, where he spoke and I learned.

"I don't know... I guess I'm kinda Buddhist but my own form of it. I believe there was a greater power that created the universe. I don't think reincarnation is real. I think that we're just species in space and we're here and that's it and we can do what we want or do nothing at all. Death is inevitable. I know that's dark but it's not in my mind. I'm content with it. I except we get a little amount of time, and we can do what we want with it, but I think it's humbling to know that time will wash away whatever legacies we think we may leave here. Everyone thinks they're special, they think they're gonna make a difference. We all have this abstract illusion that what we do matters and when we're gone, people will remember us. You want to leave your mark? Go toss a plastic bottle in the woods, it'll hang around far longer than anything else that you do here will."

"When you say it like that, it does sound depressing though," I told him, and what he said really manifested in me. We were just here for a small time. There were so many here before us and will be so many after us. Humbling but depressing. Then I asked, "What do you think comes next?"

"Well. I think roaming around in a city with golden streets would be pretty sick. But realistically, I think that we'll go back to where we came from, the ground. We're a pretty stupid species to think that we're anything special. Yes, we're the most advanced species on our planet but we're just a needle in a cosmic haystack." Every word he said wowed me.

He continued, "Every single cell and atom in us is just leftover from life before. I actually think that's the coolest part, millions of years before parts of me could have been a dinosaur or from a different galaxy. Don't take what I said earlier about god negatively. I accept that I'm here and I'm going to die, and being here for a little is better than not being here at all, I'm just saying we're just a small piece of the big picture so thinking that we have some god who truly cares about us is a stretch. I used to think there wasn't any purpose, but since I've met you and I've discovered what love feels like, I think I am here for a reason. For you."

"I feel the same way," I told him.

"Alright, enough of this. Let's go get some food."

"Yes please," I said, putting the Bible back onto his shelf.

"You know. You can come to me about anything, right? Like I'd always take the truth from you over finding out from somebody else. If we don't have trust then this is all for nothing." What. Why would he say that? He knows. He definitely knows but how? It was hours ago.

"Yeah, I know that. Where'd that come from?" I asked.

"Just wanna make sure you know that," he told me.
I might as well come clean before it gets worse. I didn't think I could actually get the words out of my mouth. How could I look at him and tell him another person was inside of me. The hurt and embarrassment on his face would be too much for me.

"Look," I said. "Last night, I was—

"I know," he said, a tear conjured in the corner of his eye.

I fell into him weeping.

"I'm so sorry, Atlas. I'm so so sorry. It meant nothing I promise it was a mistake."
He looked at me and put his hand over my mouth.

"It's okay. I don't even wanna talk about it. I forgive you, just please think about me. How would your heart feel if you found that out?"
My heart didn't feel good to start with. I was embarrassed at how much better he was than me. I cheated and he understood, he didn't question. I don't know why he didn't question, he had every right. Maybe he could see it in my eyes. Even crazier is how he knew, but I didn't want to ask or bring any attention to it. I just wanted to go home and cry and think and cry. We didn't say a word on the way to my house; he dropped me off and kissed me goodbye. His kiss was laced with confusion, and mine with regret.
I walked in and Miss Josefina was cleaning the living room, she told me that she hadn't seen Tommy Lee since he left last night, which was right after Kennedy picked me up. I lay in bed and questioned myself for the rest of the day. It was something I wanted to take back; I would've given anything to. I got into my head pretty bad, and soon I was hyperventilating and wiggling my toes again. But that wasn't working. I called Kennedy to see if she would come over and bring some of the pills. She said she'd be right over.

CHAPTER NINE

School that week was stressful. Word was starting to get around that Dizzy and I hooked up. I was a thousand and six percent sure that Alexis told, but how? Did she tell Atlas? Or did word just spread that quickly? I thought Richmont Caramel was bad. You could throw your McDonald's wrapper out your car window, and an hour later the whole town would be outside of your house with pitchforks and anti-littering signs trying to crucify you.

That Wednesday I woke up feeling like something was off, or that I had forgotten something. I was very anxious, but I couldn't find the source. I sat through Mr. Ravensworth's class while he explained covalent bonds for the third time because our first two tests on them were so low. Two out of three people failed. I was again engaged in a daydream of Atlas and where he was at the moment. I knew he was in pottery class, but I mean where really was he? Where was his head at? Was he thinking of ways to dump me? Let me down easy? Or should he steal Dizzy's football cleats to pack a little extra punch for when he stomps on my heart? Whichever option he chose to go with, I deserved it. I had so much pent up anger for myself. If I had just stayed on the beanbag, Dizzy would've come back with my phone eventually. If I didn't take the extra oxy. If I didn't even go over there in the first place. I wanted to explain to him the night so he could understand how it really went. Whatever rumors he heard definitely couldn't be the full story. It needed to be the true story from my mouth. I ripped a piece of paper from my notebook and picked off the small frays from the edge of the paper. He deserved a pretty note at least. I started with *"I'm sorry Atlas, for everything."* As I began to explain the oxy and the unexpected arrival of the boys, Mr. Ravensworth put his hand down on my desk.

"Miss Huston, either I am dreaming or you are the only soul in this class who is taking notes," he said taking the page from me.

"Oh," he said, "I see. As you were." Then he placed the page back on my desk gracefully and walked back to the front of the class to continue his lesson. Mr. Ravensworth was so towering, and his nose so prominent that when he stood over my desk and I looked up at him; I made contact with four eyes. Two brown on either side and two black flaring ones, hairy and containing boogers, in the middle. I tried to go back to my note but now my mind was fixed on his nose and the ecosystem it was to all sorts of bacteria. It probably had millions of little microscopic creatures crawling around, feasting and procreating more little critters. It was like a small but yet vast universe to the bacteria. Perhaps a land as vast as ours surrounded by the darkened barriers of his nose. To the bacteria, he was the god, the creator of their dimension. Then it struck me that we are no different than them. Small pieces to the cosmic puzzle like Atlas said. None of us really know where we are. For all we know, we could be bouncing around on a booger inside of our god's nose. And that god sitting on a booger inside of his god's nose. My Nose-ception theory, as I had branded it, hijacked my thoughts for the rest of the day. Atlas would have been fascinated by it. At lunch, he asked me to hang out that night. We did. He picked me up in his pearly 'stang and we rode on through the city lights, blaring our music and singing to the drivers that passed us up while we rolled in our impenetrable bubble of youth and love. I tried to talk to him about what happened a few nights before. He insisted we didn't talk about it.

"It's better that way, at least for me," he said. Maybe he didn't want to hear the details, and then he would know for sure that it was true and I wasn't the girl he thought I was. After shoving double cheeseburgers down our throats, he dropped me off, kissing me goodbye. Tommy Lee was inside and seemed to be sober, making dinner.

"What you been up to, Tom?" I asked him.

"Oh, this and that, did work on my 'puter but I was going crazy from staring at that screen, so I've just been watching mobster movies."

"You, you have any plans tonight?" I asked.

"Not that I know of, Kenny and the guys haven't texted me back about poker night yet."

"Why do you hang out with Kenny so much?"

"So many questions child. I thought that's what school was for."

"I was just thinking we haven't gone for a drive or really done anything lately."

"Maybe we can soon, I'm just busy right now. I'll call you down for dinner," he told me. Busy with what I thought? Was a bottle of Whiskey and The Godfather better than your daughter?

I went up to my room, pounding my feet up the stairs so he'd know I left. Then I crept back down to the kitchen, where he was pouring himself a drink.

"You. Are. Disgusting," I yelled.

He put the bottle behind his back, but then placed it on the counter knowing there was no use, he was caught. Not that he cared.

"Oh boo hoo. I'm not disgusting when you want money to run around with your little friends."

"My little friends? Do you even know who my friends are?"

"I don't care who they are," he said.

"Obviously. Atlas is over here every day. You wouldn't know because you're never here. You haven't even met him yet."

"Poor you, you have a boyfriend and a big house and your daddy gives you money whenever you want it."

"Oh seriously? You've spent more money on booze this week than you've given me since we got here."

"Bullshit. I'm just an ATM to you," he said.

"I'd pay back every cent with interest for you to put that stupid fucking bottle down for a day."

"What did you just say to me?"
I repeated myself.

"DON'T YOU EVER TALK TO ME LIKE THAT. I DO EVERYTHING FOR YOU. DO YOU SEE YOUR MOTHER AROUND HERE? NO."
I walked up to snatch the bottle off of the counter,

and he pushed me back. I hit my side off of the counter and fell to the ground.

"Blake," he said lunging to pick me up, "I'm so-

It was too late. I was up the steps, leaving behind me a trail of tears to my room. There was a loud smash from the kitchen and the door to the garage slammed shut. He took his Lincoln and drove off. I was scared, not that he was drinking and driving, that became a part of his daily regimen. I was scared that I was losing him and there was no way to get him to see. The divorce was hard on all of us. But all he was doing was thinking about himself. Watching my father, my best friend, spiral into a lifeless drunk was one of the most painful things I'd ever witnessed. The divorce was what it was. I'd lost one parent, but I couldn't lose them both.

I got out the bag of oxy that Kennedy gave me and popped one, then laid down on my bed, sobbing into the covers that encompassed me. Atlas sent me a Snapchat of him holding up *The Great Gatsby*, he still had on his broken watch. The caption said "Figured I'd sit down with an old friend for the night." I replied with a picture of my pillow so he couldn't see I was crying, telling him to get a new watch. He answered, "Never old sport, if I took it off, how would I know what time it was?" I replied saying that I thought it was broke, to which he answered,

"Exactly." I wasn't sure if he was saying random stuff to confuse me or if the oxy had hit me this soon. Minutes later Dizzy texted me.

"What you doin shawty?"

"Not you." I answered and put my phone down in disgust. I couldn't stop thinking about that night. Denying that I knew what I was doing and asking myself why I did it. Atlas was more than enough for me. He was just so tempting. Not him, but what he was and what surrounded him. I felt like giving in would bring me closer to the group. They all slept with each other. It's just what they did. I did too, but I didn't feel any closer, I just felt more distant from Atlas. I snapped his trust, and it eluded me why he forgave me without question. Maybe it wasn't a bad move for me, though. People were talking about me. I had climbed the ranks pretty well in a month. Walking through the halls, I was sure to hear my name or get looks from people, I was welcomed to the small parties and at the big ones, I was always around Kennedy's group. What is so wrong with me wanting to have friends anyways? So what if I want to party? This is my last year for fun and the end is coming up pretty soon. So yeah, I'm going to get everything I want out of it. I love Atlas, and I see such a beautiful future with him, but that's the future, and right now I want to have fun. He'll be here after high school is done, and I'll be right in his arms.

I went to get up and grab another oxy, but I got hung up in my covers and fell face first to the floor. I took another oxy and downed it with sink water from my bathroom. I went downstairs to the kitchen where broken glass and whiskey remnants lay on the floor, accompanied by a dent in the refrigerator door.

"I'll clean that up later, don't worry about it dear," a raspy voice spoke from the living room.

I jumped and peaked around the corner. My grandfather, Gerald Henry Hutton, sat on my couch, cross-legged, looking around. He was in a perfectly tailored suit, probably bought this morning, but he still wore the same old black circular glasses from the last time I'd seen him. I was seven.

"Pap?"

"Yes, dear?" He answered.

"What are you doing here?"

"Why, it's your father's birthday. I figured I'd fly down to visit."

"You know it's nine o'clock right?"

"This is quite a grand house you have here. I'm proud of him, this is something special. Where is he now?"

"I'm not sure Pap," I said, clenching my teeth.

"Alright then, well here, I come bearing gifts," he said, reaching into his coat pocket to pull out a check. A check? I don't even know how to write a check, let alone cash one.

"Holy shit," I said under my breath. Twelve. Thousand. Dollars.

"What? Why pap? I don't need this," I told him. But really, oh yes I did need it.

"Take it, it's a thousand for every year I haven't seen you. I'm sorry. Please just take it, and never speak of it to your father or anyone. Our secret. Tommy would be upset."

"I promise." I folded the check and tucked it into my bra for safe keeping. I was still in shock, trying to put together what was going on. The oxy wasn't helping. I sat down next to him on the couch.

"So, Blake dear. Tell me, what are your plans after school?"
I looked at him blankly. That told him all he needed to know.

"You might want to get on that. Time's a ticking. You're gonna need money to support yourself. Word of advice from somebody who knows all too well. Money isn't everything. I know everyone says it is. When I was growing up, I heard that and went 'Yeah yeah whatever,' but take it for what it is because once you get my age, the money can't bring back the person you used to wake up next to every morning. The money can't heal the broken relationships you have with your kids or go back twelve years to be

in your granddaughter's life."
He pulled out a flask and took a sip, then handed it to me. I looked at him.

"Are you serious?"

"Oh, please, don't act like you're a little angel. I grew up here too. Times were a lot different back then, though. Oh well, we can have that talk another time."

He gave me the flask, and I took a swig. Gin.

"Jesus, you took it like a champ," he said.

We broke out laughing.

Up until that point I had failed to make a major connection. The money.

"Hey, pap. Tommy always told me that he grew up poor."

"Well, in a sense he did. He had very poor parents. We had plenty of money. But that came at a big price to him. I was never around him much. I loved him, I did everything I did to support him and make him into a man, but I mistook taking care of him as supplying him with a beautiful house and nice things. Not one time did I see him play high school football here. Not once. I heard about him. He was always in the paper. But I was just always at work or out of town. He hated me for it. He'll deny it to this day, but he still refuses to even talk about sports with me, not that we talk much anymore anyways. After your grandmother passed away, I had a lot of growing up to do. Funny, sixty-eight years old and still learning."

"What do you mean?" I asked.

"Like I said earlier. You can chase the big houses and fast cars all you want, but when it's all over you'll realize how stupid and worthless all this shit is. Put your hand on your heart. That's what matters. Love. I didn't get or get enough of it, now I'm stuck with a big bank account and nothing to do with it."

We talked a while longer, took more sips, I was pretty messed up by the time he left, but I still soaked up everything he said. When Tommy Lee graduated he was pretty much on his own, my pap refused to give him a cent towards college, he told Tommy, "There's a whole world out there, but nobody's going to roll over to make room for you. You go make your place."

Tommy struggled for many years with my mother while we were growing up, trying to get financially stable. He resented my grandfather for never giving him a cent, even when he was in the pits, bouncing couch to couch right out of college. To be fair, he was right, he found his way. Sort of. Considering where he was now, I questioned if the money was worth it to Tommy Lee. We talked a bit more; he told me stories of my dad from high school, him getting arrested and the football team crashing their principal's car into the lake on the other side of the mountain then leaving riddles in his office to its location.

We finished the flask; he stood up, hugged me, told me he was here if I ever needed anything and then left. He walked out the front door to his car, and I sat in a smog of confusion and enlightenment. I was in the mood to write. I ran up the steps and grabbed my laptop, typing out a poem. Birthing the lesson of my pap's visit onto the screen. When it was finished. I looked back down over it, and titled it: *Love Yours*. I sat looking at the answer to all of my problems. Atlas was right in front of me, and yet, I had such an urge to look past him. Sometimes we know what the right answer is, but we choose the other road because we already know where the right road ends. We desire the unknown. Knowing this and basking in my own confusion and twisted thoughts, I remember Mr. Brubaker's offer. He would love this. I emailed it to him. He answered ten minutes later.

"Beautiful."

I read over it, then again, and again. But I couldn't get myself to accept and truly believe its lesson. Like when someone tells you a non-disputable fact to your face against something you believe, it just makes you stick to your beliefs more. But I knew the truth to what I had written.

Love Yours
There is no summit at the top of this mountain.
The ridges continue with more paths to more
peaks that we will inevitably never reach. We

beat on in boats anchored to the bottom of oceans that have claimed many hopeful souls. I understand hope, for why else would we wake up. We countlessly claim cycle after cycle of night and day, expecting the next one to be different and more fulfilling. We want things, nice things because somehow they will patch the emptiness that lies within us. We will never have enough, the day you reach the land of unlimited things, you will wish you never had any of them. I promise you. Love what you have. It is all you need. This peculiar world has placed us here with everything that we need, ourselves and each other. Instead of racing your opponent up the trails to see who can reach the summit first, ask them to join you. Stop and sit along the side of the mountain and look out. Rest for another cycle of sunrise and fall, watch the stars, those are where your desires lie. Breathe deep and fill yourself with the components of the earth from which you were made and will return to. It is only a matter of time. Live without limits, because time slows down for no man. One hundred and seven billion people have lived before you, and surely more will fill your place after. Undoubtedly ignoring the "grand" accomplishments you think you have achieved. So please I beg you, don't open your eyes in the morning looking forward to touching your head to your pillow in a few hours. Tomorrow is never promised and time cannot be

bought nor replaced. It will continue on at its scheduled pace, towards its ever-ongoing destination. We must not try to stop it, but instead, enjoy it for what it is. All of us are placed here with our own set of blessings.
Learn to love yours.

CHAPTER TEN

I was more than pissed off when Friday came around and Atlas approached me at lunch with a poster. A poster of my poem that I had sent to Mr. Brubaker. *Love Yours* but the author was anonymous. Anonymous or not it was still mine, and he said should I share any of my work with him it would never leave his eyes. Now the entire school was feasting their eyes upon corny sad girl Blake Hutton.

"See. I knew you were a writer, a damn good one too dude," Atlas said.

"What do you mean?"

"Oh please? You mean you haven't noticed copies of this hung up in every single hallway?"

"Every hallway?"

"Yes, every hallway."

No, I hadn't noticed them. I was a little preoccupied with my father's drunken habits, the twelve thousand dollar check at home under my pillow, the fact that Tommy Lee had lied to me about his upbringing, and that my grandfather told me he would clean up the broken glass from Tommy's hissy fit, but got up and left without doing so. Actually never mind, Josefina was supposed to come over today. Okay, that leaves one less thing on my mind. Oh, and my mother blew up my phone this morning. Six missed calls. I still couldn't bring myself to block her, but I was nearing a breakthrough. I could feel it. Sooner or later my finger would hit that block button, and I would have one less thing on my mind. Except now is when I need a mother the most, and she's off living her young hot Fabio fantasy with some scrawny prick receptionist. I was getting anxious. The sweats were hitting me hard. Of course, by the grace of Kennedy's fashion sense, I was wearing a black tube top and ripped jeans, so I had good ventilation for whatever my anxious perspiration tried to throw at me.

"I didn't write that though, Atlas."
He saw through my lies.

"Oh, you didn't? What a shame, I heard Dr. Dawson said that it had gotten out already and a few colleges were on their way to look for the 'polished adept young writer."

"Shut up," I said.
He laughed.

"But seriously, I know you wrote it; I can see into your soul. Search your feelings, young one. You know who was responsible for this work of art."

"Okay okay, but how did you know it was me? God, do other people know too?" I asked.

"Blake. C'mon. *'Breathe deep and fill yourself with the components of the earth from which you were made and will return to. It is only a matter of time. Live without limits, because time slows down for no man. One hundred and seven billion people have lived before you, and surely more will fill your place after.'* That's totally like not at all a conversation we just had. I don't know, like five days ago."

Damn. He was good.

"Alright, it is I, the polished adept young writer, but you didn't tell anybody right?"

"Your secret is safe with me, my love," he said.

I left lunch early and stormed into Mr. Brubaker's room with the poster. Oh my lord. The poster was hung up on the wall. How did I not notice it when I was in his class?

"Hey Blake, what can I do for you?" he asked.

"You can take that poster down, along with every other one in the school."

"Why would I do that?"

"Because you promised me that whatever I sent to you would go nowhere. Unless I'm missing something, the Webster's definition of nowhere does not mean on every freakin corner of the school."

"Calm down, I know you're fired up, Yes, I should have asked for your permission first. I just know you're not open to sharing your work, but a piece like this needs to be shared. You'd be doing people a disservice by keeping it to yourself. The message is great."

"Did you write it?"

"No, silly."

"Then I don't think it's your choice to do what you want with it," I said, then stormed out of the room. My anxious sweats had turned to raged filled sweats. Each drop containing one of the thousand swearing combinations I had lined up for him. I went through the school ripping down every poster I saw, but it was no use. They were everywhere. It's okay Blake, you're going to get very drunk tonight and forget about this. Except that I didn't. The party for that night had been canceled. Jack Festermore, our starting linebacker, called off the party tonight because his grandmother was sick in the hospital. I was warmed to see that some people did have a heart. But still, he could have just left us to use his house. I saw Liv later that day, she asked me what my plans were for the night now that the party was canceled and asked if I wanted to stay over with Cassandra. I told her I'd let her know,

which basically meant I'll come over if no better propositions come my way.
Atlas picked me up after school to grab food somewhere downtown. He said there was a really cool rooftop restaurant that served amazing Reuben sandwiches. Personally, the Reuben was a hit or miss to me, and I had come across far too many misses over hits, leading me to just declare the Reuben a giant miss altogether. I did not share this with Atlas. I could see the passion in his eyes when he told me about the restaurant, and I didn't want to say anything that could take away from this moment for him. We were driving through downtown when he swerved over onto the side of the road and put his hazards on. He jumped out of the car and took off down the street.

"Where are you going?" I called after him but he was already down the block.
I sat for five minutes until he hopped back into the car.

"Explain," I said. He was wheezing, trying to catch his breath.

"We were driving, and I saw an older gentleman lying on the ground with his walker down on top of him. I got him up and walked him to his house which was steps away. He said he was just walking to buy a pack of smokes."

"Aw was he okay though?" I asked.

"Yeah, it was really sad. You should've seen his house. It smelled like cat piss, his living room was empty except a wooden bench that sat in the middle of it. There were like pretzel crumbs all over the carpet. It was just sad. Made me thankful for everything I have. You could always have it worse I guess."

"Yeah, that is sad. It's okay though, preacher boy. Let's go get your Reuben."
The restaurant was beautiful. The kind where they took spot sweeping very serious. Everything was cleaned exceptionally. The sugar holders had ten packs of each sugar. Atlas got his sought after Reuben and enjoyed every second of it. I went for Fettuccine Alfredo, which was so so perfect. Our waiter was even cute. He had a sexy English accept that made me giggle every time he would refill my water and I would thank him, he would say "my pleasure" so perfectly. Before we left, Atlas tipped him a twenty and wrote "*my girlfriend thinks you're cute*" on the receipt. After, we drove around looking for something to do when he told me he was having extreme pains. He wouldn't say where, he just apologized over and over and dropped me off home. He texted me when he got home apologizing again and just said he was really sick, I said it was the damn Reuben, but he swore it wasn't, and that it was the best sandwich he'd ever had. Atlas had fallen asleep. Leaving me alone with my wandering thoughts. I had taken an oxy, just for something to do. I know I didn't have a problem with them. I hid

them from Atlas, but only because he wouldn't understand. When my anxiety flares up it's just easy to take one and calm myself down. Or when I have nothing to do and I'm sitting at home alone, I figure why not take one; it's better than sitting here sober. It was only eight and the night was still far too young to call it. I scrolled through Instagram and saw Dizzy's picture. He had committed to Florida State University. I commented telling him congrats. I couldn't get that night out of my head. How I felt with him. In my heart it was wrong, but in my head, it felt good. I texted him asking what he was up to.
"*Just chillin,*" he replied.
"*Why boo, what do you need?*"
I just needed somebody at the moment. I had sunken far into my feelings, and Atlas wasn't here for me. I called him five times, each time getting his answering machine, "Hey, It's Atlas Lightner, I rarely check my voicemails so if you need something, write me a letter, I'll probably get back to you sooner. Bye."
"*Something to do,*" I texted him back.
"*Something, or someone? ;)*"
His offer didn't sound too bad at the moment. No. That is not you, Blake. You are not this girl. Decline his offer. Now.
"*Something, I'm just bored.*"
"*Where's your boy toy at?*" he asked.
"*Zzzzzz*"

"Hmm. I'm gonna have Kennedy and Mikey over, you can slide thru. Come whenever," he said.

That was that. I grabbed my keys, took one more pill, and went downstairs to say goodbye to Tommy Lee.

"Hey, I'm headed to Atlas' for a little."

"Alright honey, need any money?" he asked.

"No thank you."

"Hey, um. I'm uh sorry about the other day."

"It's okay, it's in the past. Any plans tonight?" I prodded; he didn't have any drinks sitting out so I was a little suspicious.

"Nope, just gonna relax tonight, I'll be here when you get back," he said.

I got into my black mustang, dark as the night ahead of me, and headed to South Hills.

I texted him, *"on my way"* and he replied, *"Hold up give me a few minutes."*

I didn't give him a few minutes though, I was already driving up through the hills, into the upper neighborhoods where the castles of the upper echelon watched over the polluting light of Park Pendleton. No stars were visible above the city, which only added to the impurities of downtown. A red Mitsubishi pulled down the road from Dizzy's; it looked like somebody I'd seen before. Definitely from one of the parties.

We made eye contact, but I still couldn't pinpoint her name, shoulder-length black hair, tan, but her name escaped me. She was friends with Dizzy's, maybe she was leaving the party early. I thought that until I learned that there was no party.
The last time I stepped in their compound, toilet paper and Christmas lights were strung from the trees, and the yard was filled with drunken fleeing kids. Dizzy's parents were downstairs eating dinner. But very quietly, it was awkward. His mom was a very very pretty white girl, ex-model. His dad, a towering ex-linebacker for the Buffalo Bills. His biceps stretched the armholes of his grey polo to its limit. You could tell they didn't like each other. She was there to be taken care of, and he was there because he refused to give up half of his wealth to her. They didn't speak one word to each other, and after, his father retired to the couch to watch ESPN. It was different, seeing his house with the lights on, absent of strobe lights. The crystal chandelier in the main room invoked major awe. The paintings throughout the house were interesting. I didn't know what any of them were of, just seemed to me like somebody put paint in their mouth and spit it onto the canvas, but I knew one of those paintings could pay my entire way through college. We went upstairs to his room, which was more like a second house.

His bedroom and door to his walk-in closet sat on one side of the room while his living room suite of a sectional and recliner with a huge mounted flat screen surrounded by signed NFL jerseys sat at the other end.

"Well, what are we gonna do?" I questioned him, wondering where everyone else was.

"I texted Kennedy, she and Mikey are coming over in a little."

"How long is a little?"

"A little."

"So what until then?"

"You wanna rip the bong?" He asked.

"Uh… I'm good."

"Your loss," he said, moving to his window to blow the smoke from his bong out of it.

We sat there for a bit, it was kind of awkward because we hadn't discussed what happened at Kennedy's yet.

"So, about what happened, we haven't really talked about it…"

"We? What do you mean 'we'? What are you French? There's no we."

"Why do you have to act like that? I'm just trying to talk to you," I said.

He let out a gasp. "Look, I'm sorry, I'm just in a bad mood, my parents have been fighting and-

"It's alright," I told him, "you wanna drink till they get here? We don't have anything else to do."

"Yeah I guess I'm down, you said Adam's asleep?"

"You mean Atlas? And yes why?" I asked.

"Just wanna make sure he's not gonna beef with me." He said and left the room, coming back with a full bottle of rum. I wanted to ask him if he was alright and try to talk to him about his parents. You could see through the look on his face that when he was sober, there was always something troubling on his mind. Something he wanted to talk about, but I was too scared to ask. He had such a reputation for being an asshole, and while he definitely acted like one, he only seemed steps away from just another kid like the rest of us. We played a drinking game by listening to *Thunderstruck* and taking a shot every time they say it. It didn't take long before either of us needed help standing, and the rum and oxy combo weren't doing well on my stomach. I told him I was tapping out for a little and that I just needed to lie down, but he insisted I stay up and keep drinking with him until Kennedy and Mikey showed up. I told him to give me a minute and got up, moping to the corner to call Tommy Lee.

"Hey sunshine," he greeted me.

"Hey, where are you?" I could hear yelling in the background. He gave the most nonchalant "Shhhh" before continuing with "I stopped by Kenny's to grab my... my wallet, yuppers I'll be home soon."
I hung up.

"Pour me more," I told Dizzy. Another very stupid decision, and at the moment I was well aware of what I was doing. It didn't matter. I was pissed off at Tommy Lee and it was awkward enough at Dizzy's house alone with him, so I figured why not drink it all away? So that's exactly what I did. Our conversations when we were alone didn't hold much value. We didn't talk about really anything, just kept drinking and drinking. We were two totally different people. He was what I wanted to be. But in ways we weren't very different that night. Just two kids who wanted to be numb. It didn't take long before I blacked out. Kennedy and Mikey never showed up, I wasn't sure if they canceled or if Dizzy made it up to get me here. I had a bigger problem on my hands.

One forty-two in the morning.

I woke up. In bed next to Dizzy.

No clothes.

No self-worth.

Violated, but not by him, by myself. I began to cry. I got out of bed, shuffling back and forth, still half drunk, into his bathroom. There in his bathtub, I sat, head in between my arms, naked, crying and crying. I stumbled out of his bathroom and crawled to the bed trying to find my phone without waking him. I found my pants and put them on without underwear. They were around here somewhere. I found my phone and retreated back to the bathtub. I checked it and saw twelve missed calls from Atlas; this only left me to cry more, my heart at the bottom of my stomach. He sent me one text.

"Hey, I'm so so so so so so sorry. I was just really sick and passed out, I just woke up and saw your calls, hope everything's alright. I love you."

He sent it at twelve thirty.

Here I was again. My world felt like it was collapsing on top of me. I couldn't keep my thoughts straight, how could I do this again, after he forgave me once? He already questioned me, and now he has no choice. He'll see me for who I am, which was something I couldn't even do at the time. I, Blake Hutton, at one fifty-six, sitting at the top of the South Hills, had no fucking clue who I was or what I was doing, why I was doing it, and what I expected to happen. I felt like I was just standing on a cliff, pushing myself off of it. I couldn't stay here, so I got up and turned on the flashlight of my phone to look around his room, keeping it directly off of Dizzy not to wake him. I found my shirt lying in the entrance of his walk-

in closet, and when I went over to pick it up, I shined the light back the closet and caught a glimpse of a purple lace bralette hanging from the drawer of a dresser in the farthest back corner.
I opened the drawer to a sickening collection of underwear and bras spilling out onto the floor. No less than forty crammed in there. Bras of all sizes, colors, and designs. Underwear that smelled well… unwashed. It was grotesque. Dizzy was a sick kid. I felt like this was the beginning of a low budget horror flick. My underwear sat rolled up inside of a yellow sports bra, I picked them out, trying not to touch anything I didn't have to, and hear a crunching at the bottom of the drawer. I used my phone to dig through to the bottom where I found a brown paper bag. A brown paper bag that had a mighty weight to it when I picked it up.
A revolver and a note sat inside.
I tried not to scream when I saw it, I'd never seen a real gun before in my life, and just knowing the true destruction it could bring terrified me. I tiptoed over, shut the door of his closet, and returned to the bag I left lying on the floor. I carefully took it out, keeping it pointed away from me the entire time, a note sat in the bottom of the bag. It brought a deep chill over me, tears flooded in when I read it.

Dear Mom and Dad.
I love you.

Sometimes I wish we didn't have all of this money, this big house, there's too many rooms for us to hide from each other in. I think it ruined us. I think it ruined me. I want you to know that I love both of you with all of my heart, if you're reading this, it just means that I lost faith in myself and that you lost faith in me. I'm sorry I couldn't make you proud, it's all I've ever wanted to do and I'm sorry.
Forever your baby boy.
-Dizzy

I covered my mouth to hold in the whimpers. Who could have guessed Dizzy Thompson had trouble in paradise, it was a shock to my system, seeing him walk through the halls, his head cocked at an angle that said: "Yes I'm the shit, and who are you?" I would've never seen this. Not Dizzy. It spoke volumes to me. I couldn't leave the gun here for him. It would keep me awake at night, knowing he was only a few steps away from tragedy.

I had to keep this far away from him. I stuffed the paper in the bag and carefully put the gun it, shoving my underwear in on top and closed the door behind me. I put my shirt on and grabbed my keys, snuck out the front door, and jumped into my Mustang, its color gleaned under the forsaken city lights as I did my best to distance myself from his palace of sins. No fixated speed could outrun the imposing darkness of my actions.

When I got home, Tommy's Lincoln was gone. I was fed up with the night. I went up to my room and took another oxy to put me right to sleep. I tucked the bag far under my mattress and climbed in bed. There was a lot I had to digest, but it could wait until the morning.

CHAPTER ELEVEN

My eyes opened to the ceiling of my room. I wished upon everything that last night was a dream, just a stupid nightmare. I'd had plenty of nightmares since my first *incident* with Dizzy.

It wasn't a nightmare, however, it was just another stupid mistake I was going to have to fix. I was in my usual cacoonment of covers. Despite the arrangement of blankets, it was going to be very hard for me to spread my wings today. I was still being haunted by what I'd seen last night, and my head was splitting. Splitting from over-consumption of alcohol and regret. I just tried my best not to think about it.
I checked under my bed to make sure the bag was still in its place. It was. Just the presence of the bag chilled me to the bone. Under my mattress,

away from me, yes, but still only a short and very non-bulletproof layer away from where I slept. I couldn't imagine Dizzy, holding it in his big hands, coddling it, thinking that was the best choice for him. It made me sick so I just did my best to remove the thoughts from my head altogether. I climbed out of my covers and stumbled around my room, checking to see if I'd thrown up anywhere last night. After my room past inspection, I went to pee. Walking into the bathroom, my eyes caught a rough glimpse at a truly sorry soul.

I checked my phone later, one text from Dizzy: "*yo.*"

No thank you. I instantly worried if he had found out I took his gun. It's not like he could just come out and say "hey could I get my pistol and suicide letter back." or maybe he wanted to know if I found his disgusting… stache. I was going to have to answer him eventually. Just not right now.

    The guilt moved throughout my body slowly dismantling me from the inside out. I had to talk to somebody about it. I went into a panic thinking of how I was going to cover this up. Dizzy doesn't really talk to Atlas. Kennedy probably wouldn't find out unless Dizzy would tell her, I just had to pray that it wouldn't come up in casual conversation. Dizzy didn't do casual conversation. Which was very very good for me.

Jesus, what did I do? There was absolutely no way I could look Atlas in the eyes and tell him what I did. Again. I wouldn't be able to take the look of his heart breaking if he'd confront me after finding out from somebody else. I needed to relax. I didn't text anybody about it last night; nobody would have any way of knowing. I just had to stay on great terms with Dizzy to keep his mouth shut.

I texted Liv to see if she wanted to get lunch. She told me she'd meet me at the mall in an hour. I threw on a mini skirt with high tie up heels and finished the outfit with a black bandeau crop top. I was rushing to put my makeup on. Looking back to my first day at Park Pendleton, I'd never foreseen the day I would do a whole face of makeup. There wasn't time to do anything great with my hair so I straightened it the best that I could and threw it back into a ponytail, then put some hoops in for icing on the cake. Your bitch was ready to go.

I went down to the basement to check on Tommy Lee, but he still wasn't home from last night. Looking for your wallet my ass. I left him a voicemail telling him to call me when he got a chance. Then I grabbed two aspirin and a can of Tiger Balm for the hangover. I was in the 'stang and out of the driveway.

Traffic in downtown was flying for a Saturday, but the mall was packed and finding a parking spot only made my headache worse. I walked up to the food court and threw my purse down at a table in front of Starbucks, texting Liv to tell her where to meet me, and then I got in line to grab a bagel and vitamin water.

I sat at the table with my head in my hands, not moving for probably ten minutes before I called up Atlas to see what he was up to. He was in his jolly good mood as always, asking if I wanted to grab lunch. His voice and the tenderness of my name rolling off of his tongue made me sick. He loved to say my name; he would tell me he'd never known a name that could change his entire day in mere seconds before he met me. I told him I was meeting Olivia, and he followed up with questions of dinner or a movie. I told him to surprise me and hung up. I couldn't stop replaying his tone and how excited he was to hear my voice in my head. What made me feel worse was that he always sounded like that. His eyes widened and his voice spiked with love every time he saw or heard from me. He probably went to bed last night feeling awful for passing out early. Little did he know where I was and who I was with. I was a disappointment.

I spotted Liv walking towards me smiling. She had on some baggy mom jeans and a mustard-colored sweater. I would probably pay not to wear that outfit, but it fitted her, so I refrained from any comments. She pulled up a chair.

"Whatsup, bitchhh? You want me to grab you anything?" I asked her.

"No, I'm alright, gonna go get a sandwich in a minute. How've you been? How's Atlas?"

"Good, good, good"
We went through the whole small talk catching up thing for about ten minutes. I asked her how her friends were and she asked about mine. I found myself getting better and better at my fake laugh as she told me stories about her friends. I bet they were probably funny in the moment, but my head hurt far too much to try and imagine myself there with them. I had enough of the small talk, it was time for me to lighten my load.

"Listen." I said.

"I'm listening."

"Last night," I paused.

"Yes?"

"Dizzy picked me up."

"No."

"Yes."

"Blake you did not."

"No, listen."

"No seriously you did not, did you tell Atlas?"

I stared at her blankly

"Well, are you going to tell Atlas?"

"Just, just listen, hear it all out first, it wasn't like I was all 'yeah can't wait to cheat

tonight, gonna leave the house with the sole purpose of cheating, I love being a cheater.'"
She interrupted, "Yeah but you've done that before."

"No listen, he asked if I wanted to come over. He told me other people were probably stopping by too. He brought down some drinks while we waited, and then eventually said that nobody else was going to show up. I wanted to leave, but I was way too drunk to drive. Next thing I know we were up in his room and stuff happened. Stuff that I definitely regret, but I don't know what to do."
I was very worked up at this point.

"You have fucked up beyond fucked up mate." She told me.

"What do I do?"

"Honestly, Dizzy has the biggest mouth in the school, probably the state. It's only a matter of time before people find out, before Atlas finds out. You need to just go to him while you still can and just be honest and apologize and pray for the best. It would be different if this was the first time, or a different person, but it's not."

"I don't know if I can do that. I don't know if I can deal with his reaction when he finds out," I told her.

"I know this is the cliché thing to say here, but you probably should've thought about that before you did whatever you guys did."

"I wish you were in my position, you would've done the exact same thing, I had zero control last night I'm telling you." It crossed my mind to tell her about the bag. Somebody else had to know, I couldn't keep it weighing on me.

"You know what I don't understand?" She questioned.

"What?"

"That you have everything you need. Literally everything. What need was there for you to go to Dizzy's last night. If you wanted some sex why not just call up Atlas? If you wanted someone to drink with, why not just call up Atlas? If you want anything, why not just call up Atlas? You have this perfect God sent boyfriend who would jump through hoops for you, and it seems like you have more fun running away from him than you do spending time with him."

"You need to stop," I told her, "You don't know shit about what you're saying."

"I do though, everyone can see it. You've got a gorgeous house, you've got a gorgeous car and a gorgeous boyfriend to go along with it. What makes Dizzy so attractive to you? And if he's so great then why not be with him instead? Or is because you know he doesn't actually want you?"

"Fuck you."

"I'm serious Blake, it's not fair what you're doing to Atlas. You're asking for help, and I'm giving you the answer, but it's not what you want to hear. Go make something up, figure your way out of this, tell me how it goes. It's almost like you enjoy putting yourself into bad situations to see how things play out and it's sick. Everyone's advice goes right through you, it's like you don't want the right answer at all, you just keep doing what you want to do."

"Maybe the best answers are the ones we make up ourselves."

"Tell me how that goes for you then please," she said standing up

"Why do you care so much?"
She was extremely upset, with good reason looking back on it now.

"Because I care about you. You were the nicest girl when you came here. You've gone so downhill it's disgusting. And it happened so quick. Like what the hell are you wearing?"

"What?" I looked at my clothes and thought of what price tags were on them, thinking she was probably just jealous that my shoes were worth more than her entire outfit.

"It's just not you, Blake. That's all I'm saying, I don't like who you've become, and I'm pretty sure nobody else has. As I said, I care about you, but you up and disappeared when you got the little invite into Kennedy's club. Newsflash. None of those girls give a shit about you."

I rolled my eyes and turned my head away to dismiss her. She got up from the table and left but didn't take her bag with her. I sat thinking that not a single thing of what she said was true. What a jealous little bitch. Jealous, jealous, little bitch. She came back a minute later with her sandwich as promised and sat back down.

"You can leave," I told her. "Go hang out with your weird ass friends, tell that bull looking bitch I said hi."

"Excuse me?" she said fuming. "That 'bull looking bitch' is the best friend I've ever had. Better than you'll ever get out of Kennedy or any of those South Hill hoes you hang out with now."

"Oh please, name a difference between my new friends and yours, except that we have nicer things," I said.

"You are seriously disgusting." She looked like she was about to come across the table after me. "We get it," I said. "Sandra let you stay with her because mommy kicked you out, boohoo."

Her face was now completely red.

"Listen to me. You do not speak a word about my mother. I don't care who you think you are now. Nobody else does either. I don't care if *your* mom's a piece of shit and you want nothing to do with *you*, but you will not say a word about

mine or so help me God I'll slap that stupid fucking makeup off of your face."
Woah.

"Cassandra let me stay with her because I told my mom I was gay. So yes she kicked me out. And yes she apologized. And yes, I moved back in. Your mom's off with whoever doing whatever, and your dad's somewhere drinking his sorrows away. So please, tell me who has the better parents and better friends, despite how much they make?"
And just like that she was gone, marching down the other side of the mall. The strut of a woman who felt many pounds lighter. One thing I hated to admit, she was right, I needed to tell Atlas.

CHAPTER TWELVE

I left the mall and drove straight over to Atlas'. Screaming and yelling in the car to let out all of my frustration. I couldn't be mad at anybody but myself, it was time to come clean. I knocked on his door, his father let me in and their dog rushed up to me, circling around my leg. His mother was upstairs, and we chatted for a measly twenty seconds, just enough to get the essential "How've you been?" stuff in.
Atlas was downstairs lying on his bed, the lights off, just a lamp turned on next to his bed with a book over his face. He was reading *To Have and Have Not*. Which was ironic because after this was done, I was surely going to join the Have Not List: Boyfriend Edition. I flipped the lights on.

"Well howdy to you too," he called.

There was no easy way to do it. The words came out and surely it felt more awful than I had ever imagined them.

"I slept with Dizzy."

He looked at me, weak, the words summoned tears, but he fought them off, holding down the clump in his throat. He didn't say anything, just sat there looking at me, sizing me up.

"I'm sorry," I followed up.

He sat for a moment longer. I started crying. I started crying, and we hadn't even gotten to the bad part yet.

"It's not fair, Blake."

"I know."

"No. You say you know, and you say you're sorry, and you say all these things, but you have no idea. Not a single clue. You don't know how I feel. You don't know the thoughts that go through me."

"Well tell me," I said.

"You don't have to look at me and know that I've given myself to somebody else. Sex is something special, something we get to share. This is the shittiest feeling; nobody should have to feel this way. It's a different kind of heartbreak.

"I'm not trying to break your heart," I said, although my actions said otherwise.

"No, you're not breaking my heart, you're just making a fool of it. I gave you another chance after last time and you embarrass me with it. You act like it doesn't even phase you to cheat on me. How is it just so easy for you? I could never look at somebody the way I see you, even if I tried."

> "I don't look at him the way I look at you Atlas, it's just, he never meant anything, it was just a mistake made in the moment."

"Well, it says a lot about you and how you feel about me, that a moment of meaningless fun for you is worth a whole load of heartbreak for me."

"You act like I'm not standing right in front of you right now, apologizing."

"Your apologies are about as meaningless to me as you say his sex is with you."

"Jesus Christ, Atlas I'm sorry."

"I'm sorry doesn't undo anything. I don't wanna sit here and whine like a baby and make you apologize a thousand and one times, I just don't wanna keep feeling like this. Every time I see him, I get to be reminded. Everybody knows about it, its brought up to me daily, and I look like the idiot whose okay with it."

"I don't know what to say," I told him.

"No, you don't know what to say because you have no idea, you have no idea what it's like to kiss you, and know that somebody else just did the same. I have to live with the fact that when I hold you, it's not enough for you because you let him and whoever else hold you too. You hold other guys the way you hold me. You make other guys laugh and look into their eyes the same way you do with me. I'm not special at all to you. You can tell me you love me and that you're sorry as many different ways as you can, but the fact is that you've done what you've done and you can't change it."

I could feel it, the rope I was holding onto him with was slipping right out of my hands. If I didn't change, he would be gone, and I would be the one looking at him with somebody else. That scared me more than anything.

"What do you want, Blake?"

"You," I answered.

"No, what do *you* want? Not what do you think I want you to want."

"I just want to be happy, Atlas."

"At what cost? Does it make you happy to run around and give yourself to these assholes who don't value you? Do you actually know what it is that makes you happy?"

"YES, I *DO* ACTUALLY KNOW WHAT IT IS THAT MAKES ME HAPPY," I shouted.

He was surprised. Atlas had heard me yell maybe once or twice.

"Well, what do you want then Blake? That's a simple question, so why is it always so hard for you to answer?"
I was completely exhausted from this. I wanted to retreat to my bed and climb back into my cocoon. I said "I don't know" and that I don't want to talk about it anymore right now.

"No," he said, "that's bullshit. It's always some other time. It's always not now. It's always when you feel like it, but you never feel like it. You never let me into your world or tell me what you're thinking. You can't just keep me hanging off the edge of this cliff. I don't know if you're going to pull me back up onto it and then we'll skip away into the sunset, or if you're just going to stomp on my hands and laugh as I fall. Its bullshit, I don't deserve to have to wonder all the time."

"I'm sorry," I told him. And I honestly meant it. I could tell these words were coming from a deep, honest part of him.

He put his hand over top of mine. "I just don't get it. You expect me to be one hundred percent for you and give you all of me, but you don't want to do the same. Why are you just so afraid to make a choice? You act all scared that you're going to miss out, and I don't understand why," he let go of my hand. "Because you could just be having those experiences with me, but instead you choose a guy that doesn't care about you or the experiences he's having with you. He wants in your pants and you let him so he acts like he cares."

"That's not true, Atlas. "

"Oh it's not true? Have you ever thought about what would happen if you would've said no to him?"

The answer was no.

He kept going, "Dizzy has a phone full of girls. It would just be onto the next one. It would go 'whatever your loss, bye bye'. You're not going to get half of what you have with me from him, and you know it but you're just scared to admit it. Why?"

He was absolutely right. I was scared to admit it because he was calling me a whore. Not viciously. He was saying it in his Atlas way. But still, the root of it meant that I was a whore, and I was scared to admit it. And he was exactly right. I was being a whore, and I was scared to admit it.

He started again, "You want me to be here when you're in the mood for me. Then you want to shut me off, put me on standby so you can run around with Kennedy to go party and put on this wild act. And by the way it's not fooling me. I know you, and that's not the real you at all."

"Oh, you know me? What makes you think that? What makes you think you know the first thing about me? Who gives you the right to say anything about me?"

"Blake, stop."

"No, I'm not gonna stop, you wanna sit here and attack me."

"I'm not attacki-"

"Bullshit. Now it's my turn,"

"I'm not attacking you?" he interrupted. "I dare you to find somebody as understanding as me."

"Understanding? Oh you're understanding?"

"Yes, Blake, understanding. For Christ sakes, find someone else who would've stuck around after the first time. Please, go find someone, I'll wait."

"Fuck off," I told him.

"And yet I'm still here fighting for you." The truth of that took my breath away. The answer was obvious, he was standing right in front of me, and I knew he was the best thing for me, but I just couldn't say yes. I couldn't admit he was right about everything.

"Blake, it's you, you're my whole world, the root of everything I do."

"Oh please."

"I'm serious, since I've met you, I've been honest and upfront about everything. I've put my heart in your hands. You have complete power over me, and it's not fair, but I do it anyway because that's what you do when you love somebody. You give them all of you because you love them, but you hold so much back from me, but I'm still here fighting for you."

"Stop making me out to be the bad guy," I told him.

"No, it's not at all about you being the bad guy. It's not about who's right and who's wrong. That's not a part of love; it's about doing what brings both of us happiness. And you're what makes me happy, but I'm tired of doing this if I'm not what makes you happy."

I wanted to talk but he was going a mile a minute and I wanted to hear him out. It was kind of pleasing to hear all of this. As awful as that sounds.

He continued, "If I'm not what you want then okay, just say so and I'll leave it at that. At least I'll have an answer. I'm just getting exhausted. Are we even together at this point?"

"Yes," I told him

"So we're together but you can just drop by Dizzy's house for a quickie anytime you need one? What was going through your head last night?"

I couldn't answer him, shame had filled my heart. I felt ugly.

"Alright. I'm done," he said.

"No." Those words scared the hell out of me. A tear streaked down my face.

A second of silence passed. He thought, and I cried.

"You wouldn't know what to do if I left or moved on or something happened to me. You wouldn't know what to do if the roles were switched," he said.

Another tear streaked down my face. That told him everything he needed to know. I wouldn't cry over Dizzy or anyone else. He was the only one that could bring this out of me. He was the only one that could surface these emotions and I hated it, but it was exactly what he was saying. This is how it should be.

We should be able to have the power to tear each other down at an instant but know that we love each other too much to ever do it. There's something so poetic to that. Love is poetic. It's yin and yang. The waves of love were pushing and pulling in perfect unison, and I was drowning in them.

"Look," he said, "I've never felt so strongly about anything. You could ask anyone, they'd all call me crazy for fighting for you the way I do. You've given me every reason to walk away. But I can't. You make me the happiest. You're my girl."

He knew exactly what to say to take the ugly feeling away. I was his girl. He was my person. The one who'll always be here. He was my Atlas.

"I have nightmares about us not being together. And when I'm not having nightmares, my dreams are of us running away together, and the feeling is something from another world. The thing is, it's always you. You're in every dream I have and it has to mean something. I'm not making this shit up, Blake."

"What do you mean?"

"I mean I just feel like whatever I do it needs to be with you. This isn't stupid love-struck teenager talk. *My* feelings are real. You bring me genuine happiness. I've had stupid love-struck teenage goop, and I know that's not even close to how I feel about you. I love you, Blake."

I loved him, but he was right, there was something missing, not in him but in me. Something I wish I could go to the store and buy. I was missing commitment. It's my last year of high school, and I'm finally getting a taste of the life and popularity I've always wanted. There was still so much out there, so many parties to go to and people to meet. I hate that I thought like this, but I just wanted them to both coexist in their own worlds, separate but together through me.

"I love you too, I know I do. I just don't think I'm ready yet and that's what's getting in the way. I just need time."

"We don't have *time*."

"Atlas stop, please. I just need to figure this out."

"No, listen to me. *We* don't have *time*."

"What are you talking about?"

"I'm leaving."

"Atlas, stop. I'm telling you I'm gonna figure it out."

"No. I mean I'm leaving. And there's nothing I can do."

I looked at him. Confusion overtook my frustration.

"We're moving. My mother's treatment." Before I could even ask where he answered.

"Texas."

No.

I grabbed him, wrapping my arms around him, squeezing as hard as I could.

No.

No. No.

No. No. No. No. No. No. No.

He couldn't leave. No.

I was going to figure it out.

I know I said I was confused, but deep down I knew it was him; of course, I was going to choose him.

I choked on my tears. I tried to talk, but all that came out was a mix of spit and snot that was running down into my mouth.

He pulled me closer.

I didn't need to say anything because he knew what I was going to say.

He knew I was sorry.

And he knew I meant it.

I wiped my nose on my sleeve and buried my head as deep as I could into his chest.

I sobbed hard. "Is this for real?" I sobbed harder.

"Yes."

"Why wouldn't you tell me earlier?" I asked.

"I didn't want to upset you," he said.

Mission failed.

"I wanted you to choose for yourself. I knew that would force your hand. I just hoped you would want me as bad as I wanted you."

His voice, how genuinely hurt and upset he was, it tore me to shreds. I was a piece of shit.

I didn't say anything else; there was nothing I could say back to that.

We sat there, he wiped my tears some more until I calmed down. That was only on the outside though. My thoughts were going a mile a minute. There was no calming them down, the storm just had to die down on its own. I gathered myself in his bathroom and left.

On the way out I passed his mother, the woman who was tearing him away from me. She gave me a sort of upset forced smile that said she was sorry. She could hear everything from upstairs. They knew what I did. How I treated their son.

They were probably glad to get him away from me.

I got inside my house and slammed the door behind me. I couldn't even see where I was walking; my emotions were blacking out my sight. He couldn't be leaving. I walked right passed Tommy Lee when he asked me what was wrong and ran up to my room. I barricaded my door with a pile of dirty clothes. The last two OxyContin sat at the bottom of my bottle. And magically they were gone...into my system, but they weren't working fast enough. Everything around me spun, but not because of the pills, I was losing my entire world. He had the key to me, my whole existence, and he was taking it with him to Texas. I lay on my bed crying and crying, building a tower of used snotty tissues by my pillow. My nose was raw. I cried and cried some more, thinking of how I could fix this, how I could convince him to pack his bags and runaway with me tonight.

A loud crack against my window forced me out of bed. I walked over to the window and opened it. Sure enough, there was *my* Atlas Lightner, standing in the middle of the road with another pebble in his hand, the headlights from his white mustang, shining onto him. He dropped the pebble and picked up a sign that was sitting at his feet.

"PROM?"

I wiped the snot and tears away. "Get up here!" I yelled at him. Before I could close the window he was in my room, lifting me up in his arms, squeezing with everything he had. I cried onto his shoulder.

He apologized, "It was supposed to be a bigger surprise. I was going to have them project it onto the movie screen tonight."
Why why why was he so perfect?
We laid in bed, not speaking, there was nothing to say. He knew I was sorry and that I was going to put him before anything else now. I fell asleep on his chest while he played with my hair, twirling it around his finger like spaghetti on a fork. The silence spoke volumes for us, mending together all of the hurt I had placed on him. When I woke up later that night to pee, he was gone, but he left a notebook next to me with "I love you" scrawled across it in his famous chicken scratch fashion. We were going to be alright.

CHAPTER THIRTEEN

A knock at the front door sprung Tommy Lee from the couch. He opened the door to Atlas. He stepped outside and shut the door behind him. Oh boy, here he goes trying to pull off his tough dad with a shotgun act. The door swung open and they both entered, smiling.

"Holy shit. Pardon my French, but you look..." Atlas started.

"Damn beautiful," Tommy Lee finished. He was dressed in a black tuxedo, with a dark rose red bow tie. Classic. He was classic. Completing the look, on his wrist sat his tickless wristwatch. He insisted on having his suit tailored to be tight and fitted. He said there was nothing more cringe-worthy than seeing guys with suits that didn't fit them. My dress was slim, the same rose shade as Atlas' tie, it had the back cut out and a high slit up the middle, leaving the two bottom halves to overlap. It was jewel encrusted and just absolutely ughhh. It even got Kennedy's stamp of approval.

My hair was in a braid down the back; Kennedy's aunt was a beautician who came over to my house earlier that morning to do our hair and makeup. Tommy Lee and Atlas chatted it up for a bit before we left. It was nice to see Tommy like this. He hadn't taken a drink in what I think was six days, at least while I was awake. His entire demeanor had changed. He spoke, held conversations, showed remnants of once being an actual father and human being.

My mother had tried to text me earlier to tell me to enjoy my night. She also asked for pictures of my dress, so I sent her a picture of my dress hanging up. She didn't deserve anything more. Besides her constant outreach for contact, the weeks up to prom were pretty smooth sailing. I had exhausted my OxyContin surplus and fought off the daily urges to ask Kennedy for more. It was difficult, but eased up each day. I'd only been to two parties the last month, which was nice.

I was setting aside as much time for Atlas as I could. It was all coming together for us. We took his car to Greta Martina's, an Italian restaurant in the heart of the city. It was high class beyond high class, and my anxiety sparked up from the moment we walked in. Too many different silverware, certain ways to hold your glass and your spoon when tasting the soup. I knew he'd go all out for this, but chicken fingers and fries would have been more than appetizing for me. I still had no clue how he afforded it. He refused to let me see the bill, probably with the purpose of making sure that expensive food stayed in my stomach. The calamari was beyond phenomenal though, so good that Atlas put his rabbit cacciatore on hold to share it with me. I was so bloated after dinner that my dress felt three sizes too small. He was lucky he could undo his belt in the car and relax; meanwhile I suffocated in my crimson corset.

We reached the stadium where prom was being hosted. Park Pendleton had the largest high school football stadium in the state. It only cost taxpayers a measly thirty five million dollars. Pocket change. It was a coliseum with jumbo screens at either side of the stadium. There was matting rolled down over the field, and in the south end zone was a stage set up for the DJ; the crowning of king and queen would take place there later. It was breathtaking.

Students weren't allowed above the first tier of seating, but of course, people were finding ways to sneak up to the third tier to smoke and take shots. The entire second tier was decorated with huge inflatable balloons and streamers with lights strobing down onto the field. The jumbo screens played the music videos to the songs blaring overhead.

Word got around that the north end zone punch bowls were spiked, so me and Atlas played rock paper scissors to see who would drink and who would drive. He beat me, winning the first two and sweeping up with another win after I changed the rules to best three out of five. He let me drink anyways, insisting that he just wanted to play rock paper scissors. I told him I wasn't going to get too drunk though. I was at the punch bowls chatting with Mikey when Olivia and Cassandra came up behind me.

"You. Look. Gorgeous," Olivia squealed into my ear. It came as a major shock to me. It wasn't too long ago that she was seconds from tearing my face off in the mall food court. Now here we were.

"You guys look amazing," I said. We waited for a second, and then decided we needed to go in for a hug. It lasted a moment longer than normal, which acted as apologies from each of us. It was nice to see her and be on good terms.

"Have fun tonight guys, stay safe," I told them.

"Right back atcha mate," Cassandra told me. Then they scooped themselves cups of punch and boogied on into the pile of drunken seniors. I had to rendezvous with Atlas. The liquor was getting to me and I was in the mood to dance. We worked our way towards the front of the pile at the south end zone. It was a thousand degrees up front, maybe two. We danced like idiots, getting approval to do so from everyone that surrounded us who also danced like electrified crickets, limbs flying, wailing around, just having a good time deep in a whirlwind of tuxedos and dresses... Yes, we had a little something-something in us, but for the most part, it wasn't thrust upon us by the power of social trap house raging, it was just everyone, together, enjoying what was our last major chance to be kids together. This made me even more emotional altogether.

It had occurred to me that at one point in everyone's life, they and their friends took their last trip to the park together. They played their last game of tag, swung on the swings together for their last time, having no clue how disappointing it truly is to grow up. Now the only way to get friends together is to include the words *alcohol, weed, or party,* or all three to guarantee that people would show up. Of course, there were the promises of staying friends after school ends, but who really meant a single word of those? All that mattered was that night was for me and Atlas, and we made it ours. I made a yet another trip to the punch bowl, where I ran into Mr. Brubaker. He was in a sharp navy blue suit, cropped pants, with brown loafers.

"Hey Blake, prom what you thought it would be?"

"Yeah," I answered, "Why aren't you out there tearing it up with everyone?"

"Oh I wish, I got put on punch duty, it's a big big job I guess. Speaking of which, I've seen you and your friends take more than a few trips over here, and, now that I think about it, I think you guys smell, a little strong."

Shit. I stood there wide-eyed with my mouth open.

"I'm just kidding, have fun but please stay safe tonight, come find me if anyone needs a ride home tonight, I'm serious, secrets safe with me."

"Jesus, don't scare me like that, and okay thank you so much," I said.

"Hey, take it for what it's worth, don't grow up too fast, I'd give anything to dance at my senior prom again. Have a good night."

"Thanks, Mr. Brubaker, you too."

That only solidified my emotions. I found Atlas standing next to Sarah Walker in the pile towards the front, coincidentally a few feet from Dizzy. She gave me a forced smile, said goodbye to Atlas, and disappeared off into the mob. Dizzy tapped on me and told me I looked great, but there was a difference in his voice and the way he looked at me. He was very genuine, no ulterior motive to this compliment for once, and then he told me to have a great night. I made it to Atlas just in time for the crowning ceremony where, big surprise, Mikey and Kennedy were named prom king and queen. I was happy for her, despite the overwhelming vulgarities and boos shouted from the crowd.

We danced for a bit longer until naturally, everyone had spaced out. There was actual breathing room for a short while. The last song of the night came on, and the lights dimmed down. It was John Mayer. Slow Dancing In a Burning Room.

"You have got to be kidding me," Atlas laughed.

"The universe just loves to taunt us." But really it did. And although tonight was our calm before the storm, there was the underlying truth that soon our room would be engulfed in flames. It was in the back of both of our heads, whether we showed it or not.

Prom was a great end to the year; it pulled all of my loose ends together. Liv and I may not have returned to friends, but at least we were better than before. Dizzy, well I wasn't sure what was with Dizzy but it was a nice change. Kennedy was too ecstatic about her shiny crown. I didn't say more than a few words to her that entire night. I was okay with it though. I was okay with everything. It seemed to all be falling in place. Not once had I thought about OxyContin the entire night. I was hooked on something much stronger, and I feared the withdrawal from him far more than any of my other problems. Students poured from the front gates of the stadium, flocking to Dizzy's for what would go down as the craziest after party in Park Pendleton history. It was going to be one for the ages. I looked forward to hearing the stories, Atlas and I had different plans. He opened my car door, greeting me with a blindfold on my seat.

"You can't get in until you put it on," he said.

I sat down in the car, and then slowly put it on, just for some extra smart ass effect.

"Didn't know we had a comedian joining us tonight."

"A blindfold, huh Atlas? You stepping your freak game up tonight?"

"Easy there you little kink, don't take it off till I say so."

Which was roughly thirty minutes of sitting in the dark for me. Traffic in downtown was beyond congested. Eventually, we parked and he guided me into an elevator where we stood for a considerable amount of time. I followed him down a long corridor where he unmasked me. I stood in front of room twelve hundred and thirty-three. He let me unlock the door, leading into a gorgeous modern suite. A bucket of ice with three bottles of wine sat on the table inside. Rose petals led through the living room and back the hall. I didn't even question how he did any of this. By this point, I just learned that this was who he was. I jumped onto him, wrapping my legs around him and squeezing hard to hold back the tears, but it was too late. I had officially been registered as the biggest cry baby he'd ever met. He carried me into the room, kicking shut the door behind him.

CHAPTER FOURTEEN

Summer was bittersweet. We had decided to devote all of our time to each other. Even after that, there was nowhere near enough time. We could've packed ten years into that summer, and it would still render obsolete. The bottom line was that we needed more time.

Those three months were beyond peaceful. We had constant late nights at the cul de sac, looking out over the city, discussing its symbolic definition. The city itself was living and breathing. It already conquered the valley, and still, that wasn't enough, it continued to grow. Parking lots were paved, shops popped up, fast food drive-thrus appeared, it just kept taking and taking, never satisfied. We were accepting though, just focused on making the most of every moment.

We had made our way to Pittsburgh to see John Mayer live in concert. It was an out of body experience, no shit, his voice made Atlas seriously question the existence of god and angels. I know because I had to hear him think out loud the entire drive home.

We started the summer by making a list of everything we had to accomplish by the end. The only one we didn't accomplish was getting me accepted for college in the upcoming spring semester.

Atlas pushed me hard to figure out what I was going to do with myself. I couldn't help it, however, I just had no drive. He insisted that I would be a great English teacher, that my way with words could help kids fall in love with pages the way he fell in love with me. I told him he was corny, but he smiled anyway.

We spent many nights under the stars. He'd call out constellations while I pretended to know which ones he was talking about, and when he tried to point them out to me, I never saw anything more than dots in the sky. Towards the end of the summer, we tried to take multiple days apart from each other to try and start conditioning ourselves for the great absence ahead of us, but it was no use. Nothing was going to prepare us, all we were doing was wasting precious time. I had thought about our love and its strength before, and how it was nothing compared to the level we reached over the summer. We were doing everything for each other.

I rarely hung out with Kennedy, and I went to maybe two parties the whole summer. Me and

Liv didn't speak much, if at all after prom, it was okay though, the summer was reserved for Atlas. I had reached an enlightened stage where I began surprising him with doughnuts and coffee in the mornings or popping over at night with a movie and a tub of ice cream. I just devoted myself to doing small acts for him all the time. Of course, he did his own surprises for me like he always had, but I found myself much happier when I focused on giving to him too. I had become so obsessed with taking and receiving that I missed out on the true joy of seeing my loved ones smile. Me and Tommy Lee had begun to mend our relationship. We did our best to have more "family" dinners together during the week, although sometimes all that did was highlight the absence of mom. Regardless, we were trying, and that was better than where we were originally at. He still drank, and I did my best to sway his habits, but there was only so much I could do. I hadn't taken a pill since before prom, and I had never felt better. Summer was a true calm in the storm for us. The pieces of the puzzle were all falling into place. That, in some ways, made the end so so much more torturous.

The day had finally come. The stars of destruction had aligned. The Lightner's house in Park Pendleton had sold, and their house in Texas was ready for move in. I remember not being able to sleep the night before. Anxiety ate away at me. He was really leaving. Up until that night it just seemed like something we had discussed, but surely it would never happen. And then it did, and there was nothing I could do but watch as I had my best friend ripped from me. Despite sleeping for maybe two hours the night before, I was wide awake the day he left. It was all too surreal to me. He had stuff to take care of that morning; he wanted to make sure he was all packed so that he could spend the rest of the day with me. He texted me around three that afternoon telling me he had one more thing to take care of before he came over. Atlas still had to make a stop at, his friend, Sarah Walker's house for something *important.* Later when I asked him what it was, he just assured me that her family had always treated him well, that she was his oldest friend and she deserved a proper goodbye.

We ended the night with the most proper conclusion we could think of. We curled up together in my bed to watch *The Great Gatsby* one last time. Of course, we didn't really watch it. There was so much left to be done before he moved away. I tried to savor every moment. I had to remember the softness of his lips, how his skin felt against mine, I had to embed his natural scent into my mind. It was a comfort thing. There was just so many things I tried to cram in, but it was no use.

Eventually, the clock in my room hit twelve-thirty, his father had instructed him to be home at a quarter till one. When I told him the time, he insisted that it was wrong,

"That's not what my watch says," he said. God, did I wish we were going by the time of his watch. I told him it was time to go. He sat there looking at me.

"Atlas."

He stared.

"Atlas!"

"Sorry," he said.

"What are you doing?"

"I don't really know. Sometimes I just get caught up in you."

We walked to my front door, hand in hand. He looked at me, his eyes glistening, he was too strong to cry. I put my lips against his, pressing hard, trying to squeeze in every ounce of appreciation I had for the time he'd given me. It was more than a kiss. It was a promise. A promise to not forget about each other. How could I ever forget him? It was a promise to stay in contact. A promise to keep each other in the back of our minds throughout our daily lives. Wherever I would go, he would be with me. This would have to last us for a long time. This kiss wrapped up our story. I did a lot of shitty things to him, but at the end of the day, it was still us. Still Blake and Atlas against the world. He was still the hero that saved me at Dizzy's party, and I was still the stupid girl that fell for him over a jar of fireflies and *The Great Gatsby*.

I didn't want to think about waking up tomorrow with him on his way to Texas. Not seeing him again for a long time. The days and weeks and months to come were going to be torture, a reminder that I held the most amazing boy in my arms, and didn't truly appreciate him until the day he left. I did not deserve Atlas Lightner. He was meant for something far more special than me. A handcrafted angel sent to show me love. It never hit me how much I was going to miss his goofy smile, and bald head, and jokes, and his jaw, and his eyes, and the way his hands got sweaty after I held his for so long, and the car drives, and blasting music, and sitting in the car outside my house for an hour before saying goodbye every night. I took every part of him for granted.

"All good things come to an end," he said.

I hated the truth to that.

"We're always gonna have memories and were still going to talk every day. We'll be fine," he said after.

I prayed there was truth to that

"We'll make it work," I told him. "You're too good to go to waste.

These disappointments are just here to show us how much we should appreciate every moment

together. And when I come back we're gonna have a whole new love for each other."
Even in the midst of heartbreak, Atlas Lightner was still finding a way to look at the bright side. His mother might die in the months to come, and this was his only chance to keep her, so I was excited for his chance to keep her. I just wish I got a chance to keep him. He saw through me, in his intuitive Atlas way. My gritting of teeth and swallowing of the burning lump in the back of my throat wasn't enough to keep the tears away.

"It's okay to not be okay, Blake. Whether I look like it or not, I'm really really not okay right now either."

"I know. I hate trying to be strong," I said, burying my head deeper into his chest.

"Are you familiar with Aristophanes?" he asked.

"Not the time for a history lesson, love."

"No just listen. He said that when we were created, we were two people in one. We had two heads, four arms, four legs, I had my… aux cord, and you had your… well, your aux port."

"Why, just why?" I said, my tears mixing with laughter.

He continued, "We were two people in one, and when Zeus became mad with us, he split us in two, taking us away from our other half, leaving us to search the earth for our soul mates. Seven billion people, most of them will never get their chance to find their other half. I think instead of resenting however long it is until we see each other again. We just try to be thankful that we experienced even a few months with each other."

"Damn it why do you have to be so special? I love you."

"I love you too. Listen, this won't be forever, were gonna be alright, we have to speak it into existence, the law of attraction ain't no joke man."

"I know it's not, it's just gonna be so hard."

"And that's what's going to make it so worth it. Say it, were gonna be okay."

"We're gonna be okay," I said.

"We're gonna be okay," he said, kissing my forehead.

His father texted him telling him it was time to get home. I walked him to the front door. It was pouring outside, the rain coming down hard, thunder echoed high overhead of Park Pendleton. It was Zeus, upset that we had found out his dirty little secret, and that we had our own plan to beat it.

I offered him an umbrella to get to his car. He could give it back to me the next time we were together, it could be his own little reminder sitting in the corner of his room so no matter what, he couldn't forget about me. He declined, giving me another deep kiss and running out the front door to his Mustang that gleamed under the moon, without his shoes.

"Keep them," He called out as he hopped in and out of the rain puddles, socks soaked, making as much commotion as he could. "Don't worry, I'll be back for them."
I went upstairs and laid in bed with his shoes, where I cried myself to sleep.

CHAPTER FIFTEEN

Atlas texted me after they finished the move, sending me pictures of the new house, and the neighborhood around it. Texas was… well, not like Park Pendleton. But he seemed to like the house and assured me his mother loved it, so I guess that's all that mattered. The house was a small stone cottage that sat tucked back in at the end of a long winding neighborhood. There was a large tree in the corner of the front yard that hung a tire swing; Atlas said that was his favorite part. He called me on the swing later, where we got into a debate about which John Green book was the best plot-wise, after agreeing to disagree, we talked a bit more about anything we could think of. It was a weird feeling, knowing that we could talk and I could still hear his voice, but only over the phone. And that was the only place I was going to be hearing it for a while. Our conversation ended abruptly when his mother called him inside to help rearrange his room.

Kennedy picked me up later and took me back to her house where Mikey and Dizzy were. This was not the start of relapse for me, as far as I was concerned, me and Atlas were still together. Dizzy was actually pretty cool that night, he was funnier than usual. They drank and I had a few shots, but I was determined to keep control over myself.

When they busted the oxy out, I locked my mouth shut and flushed the key down her toilet. It was a nice change for a minute, not that I regretted a single second of my summer with Atlas, but I had almost forgotten how fun it was to be with other people and be a little numb. Later into the night, Kennedy ran to McDonald's to grab us food, mostly her and Dizzy as they were suffering from a severe case of the munchies. She was a little too high, and we worried for her, she walked right out of the house without her phone.

Mikey insisted I help him into her phone to check her messages. He was for sure that she was cheating on him. Which, I mean come on, its Kennedy, of course she was cheating on you man. We scrolled down through the messages; guy after guy popped up, Kennedy had offered them quick hookups in exchange for drugs. Mikey sat, hugging me, crying on my shoulder.

"I never ever saw this coming."
I didn't know if it was the alcohol making him emotional or if he was just that damn stupid. We scrolled down further to a few months ago. Atlas Lightner. What was she doing texting him?

"*Hey Atlas, I know we've never really talked but I just thought you should know I had a little get together last night and Blake was over. I was with my friends and she and Dizzy insisted on sneaking off into my guest room. I don't know how many times I told them to stop and that Blake should think about what she was doing, but I guess it just didn't matter to her. Anyways, just thought you should know. Bye.*"

He didn't even reply to her. That little bitch. This entire time I had thought it was Alexis. My best friend was responsible for everything the entire time. She set Atlas' heartbreak into motion.
Mikey and I waited on her bed for her to get back. She stumbled through the door twenty minutes later, giving us more than enough time to plan out our confrontation; he was going to let me go first. After twenty minutes of planning, it all went to waste; the moment she walked in I was taken over with anger.

"Explain this, now!" I screamed at her.
"Haha explain what, hun?"

I shoved the messages in her face. This was a bit of an awkward situation for Dizzy to sit through, so he decided to wait in the bathroom and when the dust and punches had settled, we were going to Uber home together.

"Ohhh, explain that. Whoopsies. I guess we all had a little too much to drink that night, am I right?"

"No, you're not right, that wasn't your place at all," I said.

"Oh get over it, you'll thank me later. I told you from the start you could do so much better than him. Blake get it through your head. He. Is. A. Nobody!"

"Shut up! Don't you EVER say something like that again," I screamed. Mikey sat in horror, a little on edge thinking he was going to be in the middle of a three-round lightweight fight.

"What is wrong with you Blakey? He's a loser, it's time to get over him. What makes him so special anyway?"

I bit my tongue. She didn't deserve to know. I was scared, if I revealed to her even a quarter of what made him so perfect, she would want him too. I gathered my stuff.

"Blake?"

Dammit, I couldn't find my coat; it was ruining the tension and drama of the moment.

"Blake where are you going?" she questioned.

I had all of my stuff together and Dizzy and I sat on her front porch until the Uber had pulled up.

We could hear Mikey and Kennedy screaming from out front.

The ride home was quiet. Dizzy told the driver to take me home first even though he lived a minute away and said he would tip him a little something extra for the inconvenience. He broke the silence after he became exhausted from watching other cars drive past us.

"Hey, the last time you were over," he started. "It's okay, we don't have to talk about it, Diz, some things are just better left buried, like this for example. In a way I wish I'd never found those messages."

I liked living in my own little world where friends aren't fake and try to sabotage your relationship. I knew it was jealousy. But jealousy of what? She had everything she could have ever wanted.

"No, I think we should *talk* talk. I just, there's something we need to talk about."

He knew. The stash. The gun. The letter. He knew I had found all of it. He wouldn't ask me about it though. That would be too forward. And he didn't know for sure if I found it. I would be fine, just deny till you die Blake. Which, to be fair, could have been in the back of that very Uber.

We pulled up into my neighborhood so I told him it was a talk for another time, he was a little upset but oh well, whatever he was going to say, I didn't want to stick around for it.

"I like your house, shit's nice bro."
"Thanks," I said.

I got out and thanked the Uber driver. Tommy Lee wasn't home, but it was what it was. You reach a point where you can only fight for something so much. If he wanted better for himself, he needed to do something about it. Clearly he didn't. I took my makeup off and went to bed. Atlas' shoes still sat in the corner of my room. I wore them around for a little bit, comforted by the idea that he once stood in them. It was all I had to stay connected. I sat in my bed, unlacing and re-lacing them over and over until I fell asleep.

My eyes hopped from tree to tree up the side of the mountains. The trees blended from a lovely earthy green to a frost that took hold of the tops of the mountain range that ran all around me. Up at the top, so pure and untouched, the snow and ice covered the trees in uninformed white delight. One tree stood out from the dying crystalized branches of the others. No snow lay on it. It glowed bright and lively at the very top of the mountain. I rolled down my window, taking my eyes off of the road; he reached over, putting his hand on my leg.

"What are you looking at, love?" his voice so tender. I looked back to him, nobody sat beside me, just a shadow, the imprint of him on my seat.

I woke up in a sweat, wondering where I was. Just a dream. I texted Atlas goodnight and fell back asleep.

For the next two weeks, Atlas and I stayed in close contact, facetiming every day, falling asleep on the phone together, all that good stuff. There would be days where he attended appointments with his mom and we didn't talk much, but for the most part, we were glued to our phones. Kennedy had decided to take a year off. She decided her and her one gay maid uncle were going to start their own clothing brand. You know, stuff those rich girls with infinite funds do on nights when they're bored.

I thought a lot about college. I had no clue what I was going to do, and I was still living off of the check from my pap. I went over to Kennedy's and she apologized for everything, it was what it was, that was my new life motto. I just didn't have the energy to be upset and fight with people. She gave me a bottle full of oxy as a gift for trying to rip apart my relationship. I wasn't sure if I should take it. But who was I kidding? Of course I was going to take it. I promised myself that I wasn't going to go crazy, just take one to get my day started, and when they ran out, that would be the end of it.

Tommy Lee wasn't home, what a surprise, and he left his whiskey cabinet open, so I helped myself.

I sat in his chair, drinking straight out of the bottle. I was exhausted. Atlas was gone, I had nowhere to go, no actual home anymore.
Later, I stumbled up to my room and grabbed the bag from under my mattress, reading over Dizzy's letter. I used to think he was insane for thinking that revolver was his only way out. How ignorant I was. The longer I thought about it, the more I realized it was the only way out. Some people wake up, only to go back to sleep. That was a role I was starting to fall into. We're all alone in some ways. Kennedy might have her money to lie in, Dizzy might have his scholarships to keep him warm at night, but that was all they had going for them. And still, they seemed so unhappy in their own ways. I had always thought that their grass was greener. I realized that the world we are looking for only exists from the outside. If we choose to travel down the path of desire, we flip over our hourglass of hope. Next follows the jumping from want to want, running through and smashing up all the things we touch, ever so selfishly until our time is up. At that point, we are presented with a mirror and two doorways. One of which, holds the stale and unfulfilling option to rinse and repeat.
I regretted all of the time wasted at parties when I could have been with Atlas. I chased superficial

things, and now all of the "fun" that it had brought me was evaporated.

I thought more about what it was worth. Atlas' mother could be in treatment for forever. He could never come home. He could end up liking it down there, meet a girl who was sold on him, didn't question him, and gave him everything I should have. Maybe that was best for him. I held the revolver in my hands. Looking only slightly into the barrel, I was still scared of it. Its eye was so menacing.

A cyclops, a transporter to the unknown. I put it back in the bag and tucked it under my mattress. The pills sat on my bed, next to his pair of shoes. At least that was an addiction I could feed, fulfillment is better than desire, at least the way I saw it. He was aware of the danger in the abundance of love he gave me. He didn't care though; he gave it to me anyway. That only made me want him more and now I was here, with none of him. I felt a force; it gripped me, tethered deep into my thoughts. I wanted more pills. That's what it told me. My hurt was only temporary because I was going to take more pills and make it go away.

I grabbed the bottle and took them down to the basement, and sat in Tommy Lee's chair. One pill. Two. Three pill. Five. I made a game of it. I didn't care what came next. I took another, then turned music on my phone and sat, soaking in my

tears. I took one more, they say seven is a lucky number.
It hit me.
Hard.
I was numb, my legs and my arms couldn't move. It was too hard to even properly think. I just sat and let my thoughts roam. It was so so peaceful. I reached for the bottle, lunging a couple times before I actually touched it. It fell to the floor and spilled out onto the ground. I slithered off of the chair and onto the ground, crawling to one of the pills and placing my lips over it, swallowing it dry. I was an embarrassment. I couldn't move at all anymore. I didn't want to ever have to move again. I fought to keep my eyes open, but eventually gave up; drifting off into euphoria, praying that I wouldn't wake up tomorrow.

CHAPTER SIXTEEN

One month had passed since I woke up on that floor, disappointed and defeated. It was selfish; I hadn't considered what Atlas would do if something would've happened to me that night. Tommy Lee had already lost one girl. The hurt I would cause him could've possibly struck him dead on the spot. It was a selfish and stupid thing to do.

Atlas and I had continued our daily texting and nightly facetime calls up until two days ago. Each of the last two days, he had messaged me saying he was busy, and that was all.

I felt a weird imbalance in my stomach. The feeling you get when you feel yourself drifting apart from someone and you don't know how to fix it, or if you even can. You just know you're drifting and something needs to be done about it. That something could wait until tomorrow, or actually two days from now, Kennedy and I planned a whole weekend together.

Mikey invited us to his friend's cabin rager tonight, and then we were supposed to hit up a party that Kennedy had got invited to by some guy she had met on Twitter through promoting her new clothing brand. Attending random parties you find out about over social media was really my niche, but she insisted it wasn't the first time she'd done it. I wasn't sure if that was supposed to make me feel any better about the situation or what? Regardless, it didn't.

We hit the highway for a while before taking an exit and turning up and down back roads for a little over thirty minutes, making the whole trip about two hours. We pulled up to a long driveway, with cars on both sides in the yard up to the cabin. We had our music blasting as we pulled up, but the music from the cabin still overtook our car. Mikey and his friends were inside playing beer pong.

The cabin consisted of a small kitchen, the main living room with a stair set that took you up to an overlooking loft. From the living room, there was a small hallway that led to two bedrooms that were off limits and a small bathroom reserved for five-minute puking sessions. If you were caught in there for any longer you got dragged back out to the party and forced to wash the puke out of your mouth with a beer bong. Most of the people were football players and cheerleaders from Mikey's college. Kennedy and I blended right in. Mikey and the team kicker played a championship pong game; loser had to do a dare chosen by the entire party. The kicker crumbled under the pressure. The girls standing behind Mikey, flashing him on every throw, might have thrown him off too. After his loss, he had to sit in the shower until we chose his punishment. He had to either chug an entire handle of fireball, vodka, and beers mixed in or jump from the loft onto the pong table in a glorious wrestler fashion. Considering the state he was in, we all understood when he passed up on the drinking. He climbed out onto the other side of the loft railing and we counted him down.

"THREE."
"TWO."
"ONE."
"JUMP! JUMP! JUMP!"

He leaped from the railing, legs flailing and screaming, crashing down into the table, splitting it clean in half. The party erupted, the music turned back on, and we danced on around him while he lay underneath the table pieces. Nobody checked on him. We danced for what seemed like hours but when we stepped outside to catch some fresh air, our phones said it was only just past midnight.

A car pulled up the driveway and parked right in the middle of it, blocking most of the cars from getting out. Four guys, all tall, got out and ran up to us.

"I hope we're not too late," said the most handsome boy out of the group.
He had dark curly hair with a stubble growing in on his face. He wore a North Face jacket and tight khakis. Definitely a frat boy. We led him inside while the other boys went back to the car to grab more cases of beer. He stuck around with me and Kennedy, even after we got inside, following me through the crowd. I tried to lose him but he was locked on me so I turned and started dancing on the closest guy too me.

"Sorry, babe. My girlfriend's here," he said.

"Here, bro, she's all yours." Then he passed me over to the very guy I was trying to get away from. He was cute though, very cute, but he seemed like a carbon copy of every guy here, and the whole following me but not trying to talk to me act was just making me feel even more uncomfortable. I started dancing on him out of sheer pity. I mean I'm a firm believer that persistence should be rewarded, so I let him have his fun. We danced for a couple of songs then he grabbed my hand and led me to the kitchen to get more drinks. I checked my phone, still no texts from Atlas. He was probably asleep, but normally he would say goodnight or something. He cracked me a beer and tried to make small talk with me.

"So where do you go to school?" he asked. I figured I'd never see the guy again so why not have fun with it?

"School? Oh I don't go to school, buddy."

"Oh, you're taking a year off, that's cool too."

"No," I said. "I'm a writer. Are you serious? You don't recognize me?"

"Wait what?"

"Dude, you came to a party at *my* cabin and don't even know who I am?" He was so confused.

"What do you mean? My boy said that this was his bro's place."

"Well, your boy has it all wrong. You seriously don't recognize me? I'm Alice Moody." Yes, I am well aware that I stole Hank Moody's last name from Californication, and I intended to also steal his entire career for the purpose of confusing this hopeless frat boy.

"Ohhhh, yeah rings a bell."
Oh please, buddy, I bet it does.

"Oh does it?" I questioned. "What book of mine just came out?"

"God, the um, It slipped my mind, but me and my bros were just at the bookstore the other day, they had one of those tables set up for it, I totally remember seeing your name on the cover."

"Was it the red cover?" I asked.

"Yeah, that's the one!"

No, it wasn't.

"Wow that's totally sick! I've never met a writer before. So like, how many Instagram followers are you packing?"

"Well, after the movie for my last book came out, I gained a lot. I think I'm up to like one point two right now."

"Dude! That is sick, I can't wait to tell all of my homies that I got to meet you."

"Play your cards right and you can tell them you did more than meet me," I said. His mouth hung wide open.

"Damn. So, like, you wanna go dance some more?"

We headed back into the masses when a knock on the front door echoed throughout the house. Somebody yelled to cut the music. The knock came again, this time more violently.

"OPEN UP!" A strong voice called.

"Shit! It's the cops!" somebody yelled.

The party scattered. The knocks became all out pounding. People ran up into the loft and started hiding behind couches. I saw two girls take off into the bathroom; others ran back the hall and crowded into the bedrooms.

The kicker was still passed out under the table in the living room. Kennedy found me and grabbed my hand, leading me back into the second bedroom where Mikey and some of the other football players were. One of the guys got onto the bed and punched out the window over top of it, clearing out all of the glass. His hand started bleeding bad. The players in the bedroom were all freaking out.

"Why would they even come here? We're in the middle of nowhere," someone said.

"Alright," Mikey started as he got up onto the bed, "the two girls get out first then we'll follow."

There was screaming from the living room, the cops had gotten in. We hurried out the window, trying not to get cut, but Kennedy's shorts snagged on a shard of glass and tore a hole down the back leaving her butt exposed. The lights shone off of the trees surrounding the cabin, red and blue everywhere. Kennedy and I got out. Mikey told us to just make a run for it and call him to meet up. We took off through the woods, circling around the cabin back behind where the three cop cars were, blocking off the driveway. Kennedy refused to leave until Mikey got out so we sat tight in the woods, ducking down behind trees. Two cops came back out of the house to look into the cars. I reached for my phone but it wasn't in my pocket.

"Kennedy," I whispered.
"Huh?"
"Please tell me you have my phone."
She didn't, so we backtracked through where we thought we ran, but we were beyond drunk and ended up in a completely different spot. We snuck back up to the tree line by the bedroom window. Nobody else was climbing out, but there were still cops yelling from inside of the cabin.
"Blake, I have to go find Mikey."
"Just wait up, we have to find my phone."
"Relax, you can get another one. We just have to get out of here."
I couldn't get another one though. I had the strangest feeling that Atlas had texted me and I needed to read it.

"Seriously, I'm going to find Mikey. Come on, Blake."
"No, just help me find it. I dropped it like right here somewhere."
She took off through the woods without me. I crawled through the woods a bit longer before I heard a ringing. My phone was sitting right underneath the window, lit up and ringing loud. I took off in a sprint for it, scooping it up as I ran. An officer behind me yelled for me to stop, but I just kept moving my feet. Left foot, right foot. My lungs were on fire, but I wasn't stopping for anything. The footsteps crunching the branches

behind me gained on me, tackling me to the ground, pushing my face into the dirt.
They took me back to one of their squad cars to questioned me, asking why I would run and if I had anything to drink. They breathalyzed me, and I blew much higher than the legal limit. I sat in the back of the car with another girl and the kid who wouldn't stop following me earlier.
"Alice," he said, "well I guess you were right. I'll get to tell my bros I got arrested with you too."
Great.
The officer walked passed his side with the window down.

"S'cuse me," he said to the officer, "you got a smoke on you?"

"Funny guy," the officer said back.

We drove to the station which was a very quiet thirty-minute drive. I sobered up real quick. There we were processed, photographed, and fingerprinted. The girl in the car with us was under eighteen so she got off a lot easier. She was crying a lot. They put us in a cell with four other kids from the party, one of which being the kicker. What a night he probably had.
The boy with the curly hair finally introduced himself to me as Aaron, and kept wanting to talk. I don't know how he could want to talk, we had just gotten arrested and he was acting like this was social hour. I was absolutely sick in my

stomach. I wondered if I would get in more trouble for running.
One by one through the night, the kids had gotten picked up by parents. Soon it was just me and my thoughts in the cell. One of the officers told me that they had spoken to my father. He said to leave me there for the night. The emotions funneled in, he really chose to leave me in there. The difference between him and any other parent is that instead of leaving me in there to teach me a lesson, he did it because he was probably too lazy to get up off of his damn chair or leave whatever bar he was at with Kenny. I did my best not to cry, but it came out anyways. I was tired of trying to be strong and look okay. I had to keep a big smile on for everyone who looked at me and hold it until they looked away. It was exhausting. All I wanted was to go back to that last night, lying in bed with Atlas, while he played with my hair, and we rub our feet together. I would've given everything to have that back. I fell asleep on that bench in the cell.
Six forty-five, an offer yelled for me to wake up, "Somebody came to get you," he told me.
I followed out to the waiting room where a blonde woman stood, sobbing into her hands. She looked up at me, it was my mother. She was the one that came for me.
"Let's go."

Once we were out of the jail she hugged me, crying, "It's alright honey, everything will be alright."
I cry at everything, so of course, her crying made me cry too.

"I'm sorry mom, thank you for coming."
I was expecting some sort of comment about Tommy Lee and how that showed what kind of father he was, but she had nothing to say. We got in her car and drove back to Park Pendleton, and she asked me about my new life. I filled her in on Atlas, and she seemed so happy for me. Later she handed my phone back, and I hurried to see if there were any texts from him. There was none, but I figured it was still too early for him to be up. We got into the city and she ran through Dunkin to get us coffee and breakfast sandwiches. We sat in the parking lot, and she turned to me crying and apologized for everything. I told her it was okay, and while I still didn't forgive her for everything, it was okay. I had accepted it. I swore she was disgusting, and in so many ways I grew into her shoes. Not falling more than a few inches from the tree, if that. She asked me for a favor, which I was in no position to decline. She asked to go sit down at Barnes and Nobles to talk. I agreed, and we headed over there. We grabbed a table at the Starbucks inside.

"I just feel like you should hear everything from me," she said.

"I really don't want to hear it again, one time was enough for me."

"I would never speak badly about your father, but the chances are that our stories are just a bit different. What did he tell you?"

"Um, that you cheated on him with your receptionist." I was crying again. These last two months were like monsoon season on my eyes. She held my hands over the table.

"I wish it was that simple."

"I wish it was too. I wish you wouldn't have left us. You're my mother, you cheated me too."

"Honey there's so many things you don't understand, I don't even know where to begin. Your father made up a lot of lies, not just to you, but to me as well. He basically kept his financial situation a secret from me for most of our marriage. When I first met your father, he didn't have anything. I bought him clothes, I paid for the gas, when we went out to eat I would hand him the money to pay for the meal because he was too embarrassed to watch me pay. It was like that for a long time after we got married, my career started to take off, but we still struggled."

"So what happened?" I asked.

"Well," she started, "we always kept separate bank accounts, something I never questioned. One day when your grandfather was visiting it slipped up that he wrote us a very big check for our wedding gift. That was one thing your grandfather never did, so it's not like it was something that Tommy could've just forgotten to bring up. Later I learned he was hiding a lot of money from me, the amount doesn't matter, but it created a big trust issue between us."

"That doesn't justify cheating mom."

"Honey, I didn't cheat on your father. I told him I was leaving. I fell in love with somebody, somebody who treats me so well, no trust issues, just love. Like the boy you said you met. I know this might be a bit too much at the moment, but I was wondering if you'd like to meet *her* today?"

"Her?" I asked as a woman walked around from a bookshelf. She had been standing back there picking up and putting up books the entire time we were talking.

"Yes, her. Blake, this is Sam."

"It's so so nice to meet you," she said, reaching her hand out.

I shook her hand, but only because I didn't know what else to do. They had lied to me this entire time. So much anger and hatred built up for my mother, all because they couldn't tell me the truth. She just wanted to love who she loved. And while that meant I had to sacrifice our family, in a strange way that I didn't yet understand, I was alright with that. It felt like such a weight being lifted from me. This immense hate that I had carried with me for months on months had just been washed away.

That spoke to the true volumes of conversation, and how important it was to hear both sides of the story. We sat and talked a bit longer.

I got to know Sam; she was the sweetest woman I had ever met. Very intelligent and witty.

My mother drove me to my house, hugged and kissed me goodbye, and asked that we go out for lunch sometime soon. I promised her we would.

CHAPTER SEVENTEEN

Humans. We're arguably the greediest species on the planet. Other animals know their role and play into the circle of life grandly. We, however, are charged with playing god. It happens to be our favorite past time. We create bioweapons and nuclear bombs, and tear down forests; we drive other species to extinction. I think this comes from our inherent lust for power. God, do we love power, it drives men to insanity. What else could make a man mass exterminate six million Jews? Power. Say it with me. No seriously, say it with me. Power. It was designed to roll off the tongue so beautifully. It makes the hair on my arms stand up. We could all use a little extra dose of it in our day, no? Don't say you don't want it. It's better than sex, money, drugs, all of that good stuff. It outweighs it by a ton. What is at the root of power? What makes it so illustrious? So Elusive that mankind has fought wars for thousands of years to obtain it? Control.

The desire for control isn't always in everyone; we would destroy ourselves if it was. Those who want it know how pleasing it is to have even the smallest amount. It trickles down the system, first the corporations, then the politicians, then the small timers at the ground level, people like you and me. We do everything we can to have a bit of control in our lives. It's why cheaters cheat. Why have one when you can have two? You've got to risk it all, there's no fun in safety. Those were my thoughts exactly. Oh, how you think you know everything. That was until I discovered the illusion that is power and control. We try to move our pieces around the board, collecting everything we can. Sometimes we forget there's another player in the game, life, he's here for different reasons, to show us value, teach us lessons. His favorite move is mixing up the game board, making accidents happen, moving the pieces, changing the rules, and telling us to deal with it. He likes to remind us that our power is nothing to his. He doesn't like cheaters in this game very much. Sometimes he takes the piece we actually like, and moves it all the way across the board, and leaves us with the pieces we thought we liked. Then he laughs at us. "Silly girl," he says, 'I control things, not you.' And then he retreats to watch and see what we've learned. If you want my advice, invest in love, not power.

    I finished typing and set my laptop down next to me, grabbed the bottle of vodka from my nightstand and took a swig. I scrunched up my face as it went down. The bottles felt too light. I burned through it faster than I thought.

I looked around my room for something to do, expecting new things to just appear in there. Nothing. As usual. I swigged some more and got on my phone, scrolling through my Instagram feed, updating the like count on all of my pictures. The photo I put on of me and Kennedy from last Saturday had an underwhelming two hundred and something, I definitely took a hit on popularity for that post, my makeup was a little underdone and I think my teeth just looked weird from the lighting and angle. Kennedy looked great, and I was hoping that would pull in some extra likes but I guess not. Got to try harder next post.

I sent a text to her seeing if there was anything we could do on Friday, but she didn't get back to me. I ended up on Atlas' and my messages. I wasn't sure if this was an emotional train I was ready to board but I scrolled on through. After a couple minutes, I was at the goodbyes, the "*don't worry, I'm not really going anywhere*" rattled a tear lose. I took another swig.

The "*I'll be back soon and this will just be one more test that makes us stronger*" hit me even

harder. I went farther down into some of the fights. Fights that I caused of course.
Atlas where are you?
I hadn't taken an oxy for maybe a day now, but boy was it testing me. Even just one would make this night a lot better. I thought about it but fought off the urge with another sip.
Where was he? My money's on him with some other girl who he doesn't have to worry about. No trust issues. No "hey where are you?" I'm sorry, Atlas. I just wanted to hear from him again so badly. I scrolled back up to the top and typed out "*I'm sorry*", sending it, and then taking another sip before my head fell back onto the pillow. I was out in seconds. I woke up to my phone vibrating on my chest.

"Sorry for what love?"
"I'm sorry for making you leave." I replied.
"Blake, what are you talking about? I never left."

CHAPTER TWENTY

I woke up from my dream, immediately trying to put myself back in it. I didn't want to be awake anymore. I hadn't heard from Atlas in weeks. He was gone. No doubt in my mind that he moved onto a new girl, which in some ways made me happy knowing that he was happy.
The next night was rough. I had taken the last of my oxy, and then sat in my bed, scrolling through my photos of me and Atlas. Then I reread my texts. Where were you? Why couldn't you have at least let me know you chose to move on? Then I put myself in his shoes, I had done nothing but hurt him. I didn't deserve an explanation. Texas was his way out and he took it.
I thought about texting Kennedy to see if there was anything going on tonight, but I held back. I hadn't hung out with her since the night at the cabin. She had screwed me over enough times.

I decided to get up and go for a drive. It was pouring down hard outside, so I drove with my wipers on the highest setting just to see the road lines ahead of my car. I drove and drove and drove, minutes slipped into hours while I looked for answers in the endless road lines and listened for it in the pitter patter of rain on my windshield. I searched long and hard and all I had to show for it was a lot of tears and a feeling of emptiness. I was in every sense of the word psycho for Atlas. No straightjacket could hold me. The damage was done; he was in my blood, intertwined with every fiber of me. My addiction had formed, and these months without him made me crave even the smallest piece of him. We had love that formed much like a downhill snowball, each word, each kiss, each smile held immaculately more weight than before. And then the sun came out and took it all away.

I wasn't sure how much longer I could hang on like this. I pictured him off, smiling with somebody else and it absolutely drained me. It was just reaching the point in the year where it was dark by nine o'clock. My phone said ten, but I had no intention of going home until I had found what I was looking for. I thought of Dizzy, his answer, there was only one real way out. Why would I fight to stay miserable? It was like tunnel vision, that was the only way out for me.

I sped my mustang up, and then slowed down. Then I sped back up again. Feeling the way the tires moved on the slickened road underneath me. Something like this would look like... An accident.
No.
I removed that thought from my head. It didn't leave, however, by the time the song in my car had changed, I found myself zoned in on the road lines. I moved my car slightly over the doubled yellow line, then pulling back onto my side. I was all talk. I wanted a way out, but I was too scared to take the one that sat right in front of me. I passed up on the right answers all of the time, that was the biggest flaw in my design. I saw what made me happy and ran from it, like I ran from Atlas. Look where it had gotten me. The only thing I shared in common with the girl who moved to Park Pendleton her senior year was a name.
I reached a long straightaway road in between two captivating corn fields. Headlights shined from the other end of the road. I was unlikely to see anybody else on the road for a while.
Take the chance. He doesn't want you anymore. You have nothing to live for.
You don't know that, Blake. He's still out there; your green light is still burning. Find him. *Love* him.

The car drove close. I sped up and veered slightly onto the other side of the road. It happened in slow motion; I pulled into the left lane. The car honked at me. It was Sarah. Sarah Walker. Atlas' friend. I pulled my wheel back hard, spinning off of the road out into the corn. I sat, my car still off of the road, nestled into the stalks of corn. My heart was pounding, my lungs burned from breathing so deep and so fast. What the hell was wrong with me? I turned around and drove home. I pulled out front, too lazy to park back into the garage. On my front porch sat a cardboard box. It wasn't there when I left and it didn't look like a package. I walked around to see if anybody was sitting outside of my house, and then returned to my porch and carried it inside. It was light, with objects that moved all around on the inside. I opened it up on my bed to find a box of all of our memories. Atlas had sent me a box of our memories.

He was done with me.

I wasted all of my chances and he was finally done. I dug through it, everything was there. The firefly bottle and cap, our John Mayer tickets, the Metallica shirt of his that I always stole and wore around, the RJ's roofing hoodie he let me wear the night he saved me from Dizzy's, his watch. It was all in there. He had finally thrown me away. At the bottom was an envelope with pages in it. I knew exactly what it was. His final words to me, it was my Dear John letter. He had left but I still felt in every way that he was mine. Atlas must have sent this earlier in the week, but there were no shipping labels or addresses or anything on it. But still, he sent this, which means that he had moved on. Another girl laid in his arms, looked into his eyes.

I cried until my nose was raw and my throat burned from coughing. I couldn't open up the letter and read it for myself. Read that he had moved on. My light would burn out.

That was it. The events leading up to this very night, from my first day at Park Pendleton until now. Here I lay for the last few hours, destroying myself over opening his letter. And now that I've written everything out, I understand where I went wrong. I put myself before him, before everybody else, even in this very writing. I drew too deep into myself and missed out on my other half. He was with somebody else, at this very moment, and it was nobody's fault but my own. My notebook now carried all of the weight that once sat on my back, setting it down, I picked up the envelope containing Atlas' letter. And opened it up.

ATLAS' LETTER

Dear Blake,
If you're reading this, I'm not coming back for you.
It's not that I don't want to, or that I don't love you, if it was up to that, then you would be in my arms right now. In fact, you never would have left them. I need to come clean about a lot of things. You're not the only one who was unfaithful in our relationship. I lied to you, hid away a section of my life, because in some ways I was too scared to let you see the real me, the other side to Atlas Lightner.
I'm not the perfect pure boy who opened your car door and loved you unconditionally. I'm far from pure; I'm dirty, infected with the most disgusting disease of all: selfishness. I told myself that these last couple of months, I did everything for you. But behind the curtain was the one thing I couldn't do for you, which was to tell you the truth.
I'm not coming back from Texas.

I never came here for my mother.
I came here for me.
Six years ago, a tumor was discovered on my brain, and while I could get into all of the fancy medical terms, what you need to know is that it was here to stay. I fought it with everything that I had, I devoted my life to beating it, and along the way I realized this was no way to spend my one trip here on earth. I reached a point where getting out of bed to go to school was just a mere distraction from the inevitable. I had accepted my place in the universe. I thought I had lost the lottery of life; I got dealt a bum hand. And then you came along. You gave this nerdy bald boy something he had only seen in Lifetime movies. You gave me more than your friendship; you loved me and laughed with me. Yes, we had our ups and downs, but nothing you've ever done to me could amount to the lies I've told you, and for that, I apologize over and over again. You see, it was my mother who was by my side this whole time, she sacrificed her house, her finances, her hair, to make sure this was a battle her baby wouldn't have to fight alone.
We received an opportunity to take part in an experimental trial taking place at the University of MD Anderson Cancer Center. The chances of survival were little to none, but I knew that it was still better than what I had.

I also knew it was the only way I would get to see you again, and while you deserved to know the truth, I also knew there was no way you would let me out of the city.

So if you are reading this letter, and not in my arms, then I am no longer with you. As hard as this might be to hear this, and I know you'll think its bullshit, my physical body may not talk and speak and walk, but the memories of me and who I was will always be with you.

I'm leaving you this package with all of my most treasured memories of us. The cap from the jar we captured fireflies in, our John Mayer tickets, my DVD of The Great Gatsby, my *watch*, and everything else I've thrown in. These and my parents were the only company I had my last few days. I've instructed my parents to send this package to Sarah Walker, the only other person outside of my family who knew of my condition. She knows to give you this package when the time is right.

I am so sorry. Sorry I dragged you on, thinking there would be an end to this, I wanted with everything for there to be an end. Believe me. You were all I'd ever had.

I understand now. I understand so much about Gatsby that riddled me up until these last couple weeks. I had always thought if he had just tried a little harder, thrown grander parties, and said sweeter things to Daisy, he could have had her.

She was right there. His dream wasn't unreachable, he was just robbed of his chance and stopped short by Wilson. I shared hope with him. I'd always liked to think that no matter how much they paint the American dream to be a sham, it was still very real. I liked to think maybe he would've got to her sooner or later. Just as I liked to think I would have gotten to you sooner or later. I was upset for a while that, like Jay, my chance was being stolen from me. But I know that I've done everything I could've for you, and I like to think that you would've come around. Maybe I should've told you earlier, I just didn't want that to be the reason for you to choose me. I didn't want your pity, just your love.

I'm not mad at you for what you've done to me. How could I be mad?

You've let me feel alive, even if it didn't last. All good things come to an end, that's what makes them good. It didn't need to last forever, I'm just happy I got to call you mine. I hope you're thankful for me, and every memory, good or bad, is laced with love. My journey with you was beautiful; you've made me feel ways I never thought I would've.

Whether I wake up from this bad dream on an alien spaceship or I'm reincarnated or all light ceases and I'm cast off into the darkest corners of the universe as atoms and particles of dust, I promise you I'll always keep the love you've given with me. I knew the day would come when my heart would cease to beat, and all that would be left was the memories manifested in you and the way we made each other feel.

You are so beautiful and bright. I know you'll go on to take over whatever you put your mind to. Fight hard for what you want, the world is not ready for Blake Hutton, just remember that.

Thank you for the last couple of months.

I forgive you for everything, and I hope that you forgive me too.

I love you, Blake.

Yours truly,

Atlas Lightner

THE CYCLOPS

I put the letter down. I'm sorry, Atlas. For everything. I know now this won't do a thing for either of us. You're gone. Oh my God you're gone. I wish you could see me. I wish you could see my tears. You deserve to see me hurting. I can't believe I've made you feel what you've felt and hurt you the way you've hurt. I wish I could take away all of the hurt I've put on you and feel it myself. I would destroy myself for you. I'm destroyed now, but it doesn't matter. You're not coming back. Fuck I can't believe you're not coming back.

When you left, I knew you'd be gone for some time. But you promised me you were coming back. You fucking promised I'd see you again. How could you tell me that? How could you let me live with the hope that I'd get to hold you again and look into those unbelievable eyes and touch that shiny head. How could you let me think I'd get to feel your skin on mine again? You were supposed to be my green light. You kept me going and waking up every morning and carrying myself through school. I destroyed myself these last couple months.

There's no point for me to do any of this now, I kept going so that I could see you and tell you how much I've learned.

I was supposed to tell you I'm sorry.

That I mean it this time.

That I've learned and I understand what you were trying to tell me all along.

You're what I've wanted but I couldn't see it because I was in my own way. You're better than all of this. You're better than the vodka and the oxy and the parties. You're better than Kennedy. You're better than Dizzy. You're better than Park Pendleton. You're better than me.

How could you not tell me you were suffering? I don't want to even think of your last days in that bed, knowing what was to come. How could you have gone on the last year knowing what was going to come? I should have been next to you, holding your hand while you past on and left all of this behind. You were always too good for this place and you knew it. You were the light in the deep shrouding darkness. I hope you saw the good in me and were trying to get me away from this place, but how could you leave me in the dark. Did you finally realize I don't deserve you? This is all too much.

I just need to take a second and gather myself.

I sit up on my bed, looking at the box, looking at the letter that tore away from me everything that ever meant anything to me. I look at his watch. I think of him wearing it, god how handsome he was. The most beautiful soul with the most beautiful smile. The most beautiful voice, always knowing the right thing to say and how to say it. I can't stop crying, my face and my sheets are soaked through with tears that I absolutely deserved to cry.

The thoughts of him rush through my head. Too many to single out and zone in on. I'm standing along a highway of thoughts, they rush by me like cars, some beautiful and some ugly, but such is love.

They stay for an instance and are gone as others take their place.

The fireflies.

The green light.

His mustang.

His arm hanging out through the window as he pulls up to my house.

His half crooked smile he always wore that told you he knew he was special, that he always knew something you didn't. Well I guess in the end he really did.

Sitting behind all of the memories was the abhorrent image of him in that bed, writing this letter. Wires running to places, machines buzzing and beeping, the stale smell of imminent tragedy soon to take the place of whatever room number sat above the doorway outside. I hope he didn't suffer; he deserved that much, if not more. One thing I know for sure, no matter how he went, he was a gentleman about it, smiling to his nurses, saying thank you as they pumped him with chemicals and put wires where he didn't want them. A big smile on his face while the doctors wondered why and how.

He was an angel. My angel. And I threw him away. God I want him back. I WANT HIM BACK. I would say I wish I never met him, I would wish he never graced my life with so much beauty, but I can't, he was always so hopeful. Knowing why now makes me cry that much more. Atlas Gregory Lightner you are the most fucking beautiful person and I am sorry with every ounce of regret, love, and energy I have. You were the flower I saw in the winter, rooted deep and swelling with purity, holding on, while the plants and trees around you were dying of excess and immorality.

The memories of him keep flooding in, I'm trying my best to filter out the fights and focus on our good but it's no use, love is good and bad, the kisses and the yelling. Without the fighting, we wouldn't know how special the moments of laying up late at night in my bed talking about aliens or whatever curiosity occupied his thoughts for the day would be are.

It doesn't matter. The fact is that he was dead, he is dead, and he will be dead. Then, now, and forever. My memories of him serve as an annihilating testimony that time will not stop for anyone or anything, no matter the bribe. Take this for what it is. This disgusting earth that we set out to implant love and meaning in, is yet the most loveless, meaningless, corner of the universe. The sooner this is learned, the sooner all will be at peace with the grand facade we've bought into. Life is no more than a brilliantly marketed vacuum for us to get lost in and waste our time on quick pleasures until we realized the greatest pleasures of all had passed us by long ago. I can't be mad at anybody else; the choices I made were my fault.

I sit for a while on the edge of my bed, hoping sooner or later I'll run out of tears. I go back through the box of pictures and play with the cap from the firefly jar; it calms me down knowing that at one point he did the same. This all still seems like a dream to me. It doesn't seem right to think that somewhere out there his body is lying lifeless, no longer breathing and swallowing. Even during the period that I stopped hearing from him, I still knew that somewhere he was moving about, traversing the word and taking energy and giving it back, interacting and living.

Now he was giving back to the soil somewhere, his body breaking down and his energy and atoms dispersing back into the universe that made him. I know he would've liked the thought of that. He thought that shit was so cool.

It calmed me to know that if he did suffering, he wasn't anymore, but only because he passed that suffering onto me. I was praying that he was looking down on me next to his other angels or however that worked. Maybe he was even in the room with me, stroking his hand down my cheek or playing with my hair for the last time. He always told me I was a pretty crier and I hoped, despite all of the ugly I've done to him, he still thought I was as beautiful as I was the day I ruined his favorite shirt.

I want to be with him so so badly. I'll give anything for that chance. Anything. Maybe I don't deserve the chance to be with him again. Maybe this was destiny. My green light finally had blown out. He was here to show me the great and precious parts of life and I was the greed and the lust that hardens in the cracks of the soul, inevitably ruining it. Together we were the ying and the yang, the light and the dark that kept life balancing on its precious scale, never tipping too far to either side. Destiny.

Destiny was bullshit. I get to create my own destiny now.

He lied to me. He promised he would find his way back to me. If he would've left bread crumbs I would've found my way to him. He didn't though. He lied.

I tear into our memory box in a fit of rage. Ugly. I hold his stupid watch in my hands. Who the hell wears a broken watch? The light from my fan above shines through the cracks on the face. I whip it against my wall with everything I have. If he's here in the room I hope he sees that. It bounces to the floor, the back piece to the watch breaking off.

I'm sure that woke Tommy Lee up, but what was he going to do. Actually no, he probably went to sleep too drunk to wake up before noon tomorrow anyhow. My actions register in my head. His watch. What the hell was I doing? I sprang from the bed onto the floor like a fiend.

I lay overtop of it, coddling it like a crying child in a storm to his teddy bear.

His watch, I'm so sorry Atlas.

I grab the watch and the broken off back trying to put them together. They won't click back together.

My eye catches a scratch on the inside of the back piece.

Etched into the back of the watch, it reads *"THX"*. I sprawl onto the ground sobbing, "Atlas" creeps from my lips softly between the wails.

I crawl to my bed and pick up the journal, now full of my most beautiful and tragic stories. I tear as many pages out as I can, one by one, and then in bunches.

I jump up and flip my mattress to reveal a milk white bottle.

The cap comes off and the pills go down.

I promised I wouldn't, but I can't hold out. Why should I hold out? He's not here to be disappointed in me anymore.

My head is splitting, my thoughts won't stop rushing through me.

I hear a call from across the room. The *cyclops,* he torments me, calling my name and whispering my failures.

He says that there's nothing else I can do.

He says there's no way to fix this, I've destroyed my happiness, just like I destroy everything else. I've destroyed my parents' marriage, Olivia hates me, Atlas is dead, Tommy Lee is a drunk.

He says he can take the pain away, better than the pills can. He says he can do one thing the pills cant. He can let me see Atlas again.

I think he's lying, but then again how could I know? He's wise, the disruptor of balance, he creates nothing but takes everything. So enticing. I pick him up and look into his eye. He's cold, chills disperse through me. He comforts me, telling I'm smart, that I'm making the right choice, but my tears tell me otherwise.

Take me, take my sins away, take away the hurt and the regret. Take my body.

"Please" I beg him.

No.

Stop. Blake you've made mistakes but it's never too late. You need help, you're broken but fixable. When you heal a broken bone it's twice as strong as before. You have friends that love you. Apologize to Liv, she'll understand. You're just hurting, but pain is temporary. Your friends can help you through this.

"Wrong." The cyclops calls. "What friends do you have? They all hate you. Kennedy uses you, Olivia hates you, Atlas is dead. Your so called "friends" are not real. Do you see them here trying to help you? No. Only I am here to help you. The horrible rectifying truth is that these friends of which you speak of want not to see you succeed. You see, they are ruined themself. They won't help you. Instead they want to rob you for every ounce of goodness you have, they like to see you fail. They want to even the playing field, to bring you down to or below the level of emptiness which they reside on. They're just as alone and scared as you are. Nobody wants to be alone in a scary place. You choose to be alone in this scary and unforgiving place. You've chosen greed. You've chosen to speak instead of to listen, to hate and cheat instead of love. Don't you understand, Blake? Why, you've chosen to be

alone. But it's not too late, make the right choice, choose me. Choose to be free."
I looked into his eye.
He seemed honest. I think he was telling the truth. How could I be sure though?
With the deepest of burning breaths, I try to steady myself.
Counting backwards from ten. I force solace into my bullet riddled, war torn mind.
The memories are flooding in, but I hold them off the best I can.
I slam a white flag into the scarred battlefield.
Both sides surrender their hands, shocked, making no sudden movements.

    "Are we really doing this?" they ask.
The cyclops does not answer, only stares.
I wipe the tears from my face.
For once I feel in control. There is no more war.
I love you Atlas, I don't know where you are, but I hope one day our particles will meet again, and recycle into new life, making us whole again.
Just like you said.
Three.
Two.

Made in the USA
Middletown, DE
03 March 2019